B Francis

**Isles of the Pacific**

Or, Sketches from the South Seas

B Francis

**Isles of the Pacific**
*Or, Sketches from the South Seas*

ISBN/EAN: 9783743407473

Manufactured in Europe, USA, Canada, Australia, Japa

Cover: Foto ©Andreas Hilbeck / pixelio.de

Manufactured and distributed by brebook publishing software (www.brebook.com)

B Francis

**Isles of the Pacific**

THE

# ISLES OF THE PACIFIC;

OR,

## Sketches from the South Seas.

BY

## B. FRANCIS.

CASSELL & COMPANY, Limited:

*LONDON, PARIS & NEW YORK.*

1883.

# CONTENTS.

## CHAPTER VII.

## CHAPTER VIII.

## CHAPTER IX.

## CHAPTER X.

## CHAPTER XI.

# INTRODUCTORY.

THERE is something in the thought of distant islands which has always had strong attractions for the human mind. From the earliest ages they have figured in the visions of bards as favoured regions of bliss and beauty. In the prophetic utterances of the Hebrew seers the kings of the isles are described as laying their treasures at the feet of the promised Messiah—the multitude of the isles as rejoicing in Jehovah's sovereignty. When we look to the early records of Greece, we not only find her "isles" the actual cradle of law and poesy, we see also that the Greek poets sang of islands yet brighter and lovelier, to which they looked westward through a haze of mysterious legends, as scenes of nature's most lavish bounty :

" Summer isles of Eden, lying in dark purple spheres of sea."

When Homer, in his wild and wondrous "Odyssey," told of "the ever-blooming gardens of Alcinous," and the glories of joyous Phæacia, he had doubtless in view not only the rich vegetation and genial clime of Corfu, as described by travellers, but fancy pictures of happy isles beyond the pillars of Hercules, where the Hesperian fruit might be plucked without fear of the " red-combed dragon " barring the entrance to that western paradise. There is a remarkable hymn which the Athenians used to sing in memory of Harmodius and Aristogeiton, who rose against the rule of the Peisistratidæ :—"Most beloved Harmodius,"—so runs the strain—" thou art not

dead; they say thou art in the islands of the blessed,"
&c. This, again, may remind us of the ancient British
legend of King Arthur, so beautifully versified by
Mr. Tennyson, which supposes him still resting, to use
the laureate's words,

> " In the island valley of Avilion,
>   Where falls not hail, or rain, or any snow,
>   Nor ever wind blows loudly, but it lies
>   Deep-meadow'd, happy, fair with orchard-lawns
>   And bowery hollows crown'd with summer sea."

Such have been the day-dreams of the poet in many
lands. Childhood, full of unconscious poetry, revels in
stories of distant island homes, island mysteries, island
researches. Nothing in the Arabian Nights' attracts its
eager fancy more than the story of " Sindbad the
Sailor," with his strange experiences of wonder-teeming
isles. " Robinson Crusoe" will be a "fearful joy" to the
young while the English language lasts. "Sir Edward
Seward's Narrative," " Penrose's Journal," a delightful
book, now, alas! out of print, and " Masterman Ready,"
all recognised and ministered to this youthful passion
for island adventures, and all were popular accordingly.
The present volume is an attempt to convey to young
readers a fair notion of the isles of the Pacific Ocean,
of their principal clusters, and of the features which
distinguish several of the most remarkable among them.
They differ from each other so widely in climate, natural
features, social and political condition, that even a few
sketches, if tolerably faithful, will at least have the
advantage of variety; while they may also serve to clear
up a certain amount of confusion as to groups and races
which exists, I believe, in young minds generally, and is
not rare among children of a larger growth.

# THE ISLES OF THE PACIFIC.

## CHAPTER I.

### NEW ZEALAND.

The Pacific Ocean — Balboa—Magellan—New Zealand—The Maories—Vegetation—Fruit, Flowers, and Birds—Tattooing — Super-stitious Customs.

IT is strange to think of the time when the vast tract of water which we call the Pacific Ocean, and which covers nearly half the globe, with all its wonderful and beautiful islands, was unknown to the civilised world. Yet it was only in the year 1513 that its existence was discovered by a Spaniard of the name of Balboa.

This brave and patient man made his way, with the utmost toil and peril, on foot, across the isthmus which separates the Atlantic from the Pacific Ocean, and having been assured by his Indian guides that the sea

was to be seen from a certain mountain, he climbed it
all alone, and, when he reached the top, there sure
enough lay the broad ocean on the other side, its calm
waters glittering in the sun, and stretching away and
away—who could say where? No wonder that
Balboa fell on his knees in the solitude, and thanked
God for having guided him to make so great a discovery. When he at last gained the shore on the other
side of the mountain, he plunged at once into the water,
with his drawn sword in his hand, and took possession
of it in the name of his king, Ferdinand of Spain. And
that was the beginning of the discoveries of all the
treasures and wonders of the Pacific Ocean, with its
countless islands and strange inhabitants.

Seven years after Balboa's journey, Magellan, a
Portuguese, discovered the straits which now bear his
name, and, passing through them, first launched a European ship in the Southern Sea. On he sailed, across the
immense tract of calm, untraversed water, he knew not
whither. How amazed the sea-gulls and the flying-
fish must have been at the sight of the great strange object, making its way across the blue expanse! Perhaps
they took it for some gigantic bird, with huge white
wings and an enormous appetite, and fled in terror. One
would think even the little rippling waves themselves
must have been astonished at such a new sensation as
that of a ship cleaving its way among them.

Magellan discovered the Ladrone, and afterwards the
Philippine Islands. His ship, the *Victory*, performed
the first voyage ever made round the world; but the
great discoverer himself never received the thanks and
praise of his king and country, which he had so justly
earned. He was killed by the natives in one of the

Philippine Islands. Afterwards various Spanish, Dutch, and British navigators followed Magellan's adventurous course across the waters of the Pacific, and discovered other islands of the Polynesian Group, so named from a Greek word signifying "many islands." But the most important and extensive discoveries in this region were not made till the latter part of the last century.

VIEW IN THE STRAITS OF MAGELLAN.

It is curious to remember that only some hundred and fifty years ago many lands whose names are now so familiar to us were as unexplored, and, indeed unknown, to the civilised world, as the countries in the moon, if there are such, are now. Many birds and beasts which we may now see any day in the Zoological Gardens had never entered the imagination of a European. Flowers and creepers now common in our

gardens and greenhouses were utterly unknown.
Queen Anne would have been as much astonished if she
had been shown a kangaroo as we should be now if we
met Alice in Wonderland's "Mock Turtle."

Our great navigators and explorers have brought
many new objects of interest and beauty within our
reach, and have added to the comforts and luxuries of
our lives in all sorts of ways; but what far more wonderful changes the arrival of the white men and their
ships have brought to the new lands themselves, and
their more or less savage inhabitants! We have taught
them and brought them a thousand good and useful
things. It is sad to think that we have also taught
them things that are neither good nor useful, and given
them things which can only do them harm.

Of the many beautiful islands in the Pacific Ocean,
New Zealand has perhaps the greatest interest for us
English people. If we look at the globe, we shall see
that it is what is called our *antipodes*—that is, the other
side of the world, the country farthest from us of all
countries yet known to us; still, if we could land there
to-morrow we should probably feel more as if we were
still in England than we should do if we visited any other
part of the world, so completely have we filled it with our
own people, plants, and animals, and built towns and
villages almost like those in our own land. The climate,
too, is in some respects like our own, but warmer and
finer, and the atmosphere is clear and bright, and the
sky very blue. There is a slight dampness in the air,
owing, it is thought, to the vast tracts of water by
which it is surrounded, but which keeps the foilage and
the grass as green as it is in England.

Of all the islands in the world, New Zealand is

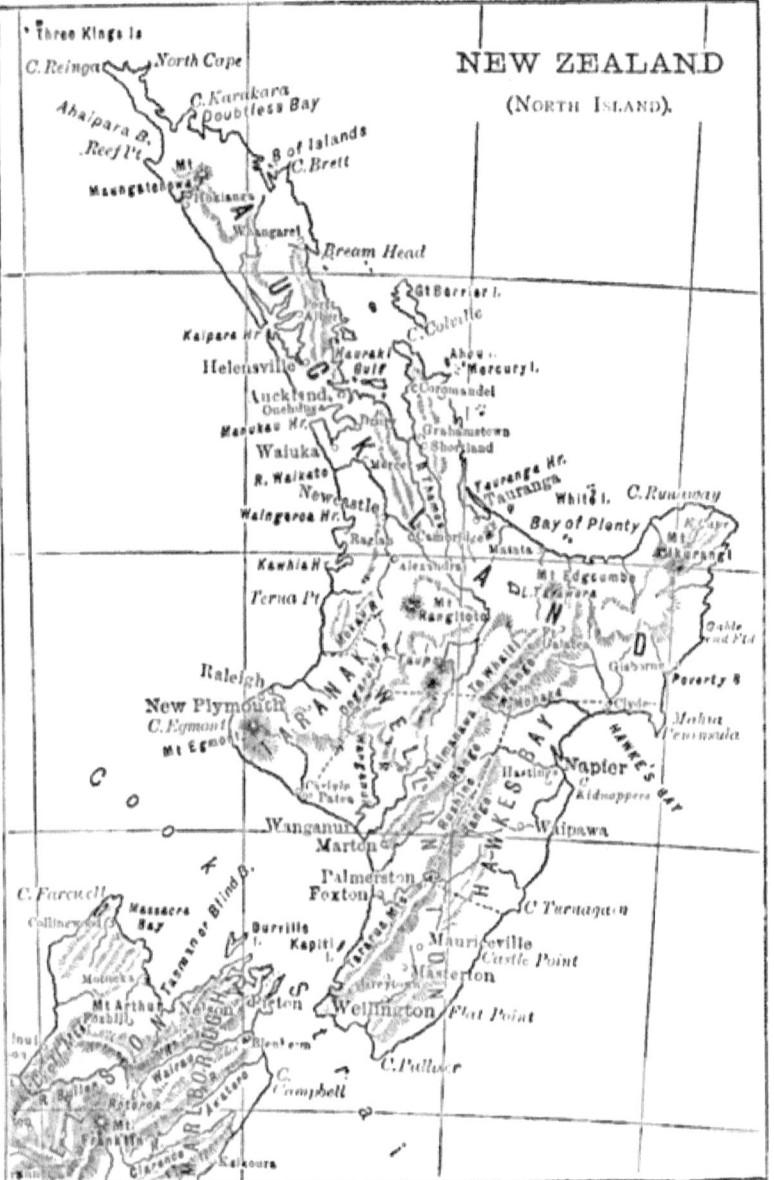

NEW ZEALAND

(NORTH ISLAND).

surrounded by the largest extent of water. The great Pacific Ocean stretches away in an unbroken sweep, on the east to South America, on the west to Australia, and north and south to the arctic and antarctic regions. The nearest land to it is, on one side the great island of Australia, about a thousand miles off, and on the other the beautiful South Sea Islands, many of whose foundations are so marvellously reared from the depths of the ocean by myriads of tiny coral insects. New Zealand was first discovered in the year 1642, by the famous Dutch navigator Abel Tasman; but the natives would not allow him to go on shore, and nothing was really known about it till Captain Cook landed there, more than a hundred years later.

Though so near Australia, it is strangely unlike it in its climate, in its plants and animals, and above all in its natives; for while the Australian aboriginals are one of the lowest of all savage tribes in appearance and mode of life, the Maories of New Zealand, supposed to have come originally from the Malay race, are a fine, intelligent tribe of men, and perhaps, in the condition in which we first found them, the most civilised in their way of living of any savage people. Captain Cook found them living together in villages, in huts made of wood and reeds. They wore clothing woven from the native flax, and dyed with bark, and they made stone weapons, and instruments of various kinds, and cooked their food. They also cultivated the land, and made laws about property, and stored provisions against bad times. Being much given to fighting among themselves, they made forts and defences of the most ingenious kind. Though they had no written language, they had all sorts of songs and proverbs, handed down from generation to generation; and they knew and had named every bird, plant, and insect in their island. They had names also for the stars, and called the constellations from fancied resemblances to different familiar objects, such as canoes or weapons. They had various games and amusements, many of them like our own—such as flying kites, walking on stilts, wrestling, and hide-and-seek.

WOMAN OF NEW ZEALAND.

They treated their wives well: in fact, we should have had no right to call them a savage race, but for a frightful custom prevailing among them, long since, thank God, given up. They were cannibals, and after a battle it was their custom to kill and eat the prisoners they had taken. This they considered a solemn duty as well as a pleasure, and they imagined that devouring their enemies would make them strong and brave in fight. They had no religion, only a sort of strange mythology of their own; but they believed in a future existence.

New Zealand properly consists of three islands. The two larger, called North and South, are about as big as

MAN OF NEW ZEALAND.

Great Britain. The little one, south of all, is too small to be of any importance. It was in the first-named island that our missionaries and colonists first established themselves.

The fruits and flowers of New Zealand are endless in variety and beauty. Besides many beautiful trees and

plants natural to the country, every sort of root and seed
introduced by Europeans has grown and flourished,
either in the north or south, in a wonderful way. In
the North Island, the myrtle and scarlet geranium
bloom unsheltered all the year round; and grapes, figs,
and melons ripen perfectly in the open air, and in the
most northern parts, oranges, bananas, and pine-apples;
but as tropical fruits of every description are to be obtained so easily from the neighbouring South Sea
Islands, it is not worth while spending the time in cultivating them.

In the fruit-markets, side by side with the products of
the hottest climates, which we never taste in their first
freshness in England, are our own currants, gooseberries,
cherries, and strawberries, which grow in the South Island
in the utmost profusion and perfection. All our English
vegetables thrive, as well as the kumera, or sweet potato,
grown by the Maories, and so do our favourite English
flowers—rose, honeysuckle, lavender, mignonette, etc.,
even snowdrops, crocuses, and daffodils. Our English
oak and elm and other trees grow well also; but for
trees and flowers New Zealand was well off before the
Europeans planted any there. A New Zealand forest
in its native wildness is a most beautiful sight, with
its infinite variety of pine-trees, evergreens, creepers,
and shrubs. Many of the large trees bear lovely
flowers, and the ground is carpeted with them. Among
the most beautiful plants are the tree-fern and the
cabbage-palm; the commonest is the manuka scrub,
which grows all over the island. It is something like a
myrtle, and has white, and sometimes pink, blossoms.
All the native trees, with one or two exceptions, are
evergreen.

B

One of the handsomest, and certainly the most useful, plants of New Zealand is a kind of flax, which grows all over the island. The natives have always used it for

all sorts of purposes, and it has a value in all countries on account of the quality of the flax. It has a very handsome large red flower, something like the *fleur-de-lis*, and has great sword-shaped leaves. It sometimes grows as high as seven feet, and in a heavy shower of rain a flax-bush makes a capital shelter. To give me an idea of the strength of the plant, a gentleman told me that he had seen a heavy boat fastened to its stem, and kept steady in a strong stream. The Maories are very fond of sucking the honey which the flowers produce. Before the Europeans came, nearly all their clothing was made from this wonderful flax, not woven, but knotted together in a peculiar manner.

The ordinary native dress is a garment of this material, nearly square, about five feet in length and four in breadth. It is fastened round the shoulders by two corners, and round the waist with a girdle. Over this they sometimes wear a large mantle covered with dog-skin. The dress of both women and men is the same. Their

CARVED BOX FOR
FEATHERS.

ornaments are feathers upon the head, and combs and pearl-shells. In their ears they wear pieces of jasper or green jade and sharks' teeth. The women adorn their necks with strings of sharks' teeth and a particular kind of berry. The feathers worn by the chiefs are considered of great importance, and in some way distinguish the different tribes to which they belong. They are kept in beautifully-carved boxes, a specimen of which is to be seen at the British Museum.

The Maories, in their natural condition, live chiefly on fish and herbs. There are no native quadrupeds in New Zealand except dogs and rats, and the former are supposed to have been originally brought from some other island. The native rat is now nearly extinct, having been destroyed by the European one. A kind of otter has been occasionally seen in the mountains. There are no snakes, and only one kind of frog, but plenty of lizards.

When Captain Cook landed among them, he found the New Zealanders living upon fish, fern-root, dogs, and rats. He introduced the kumera, or sweet potato, to them, which has since become their chief article of diet. He also presented them with some pigs, whose descendants have now become a wild race, with long snouts and long tails, and have spread all over the country. Chasing these wild pigs is a favourite sport in New Zealand. Lady Barker, in her book of "Station Life," gives a delightful description of a boar-hunt, in which her life was probably saved by her presence of mind. One of the wild pigs, or boars, charged full at her and her horse, Helen, and she dropped a large stone on his head and killed him.

There are a great variety of birds in New Zealand—

green parrots and pigeons of various kinds; the bell-bird, with its sweet, dreamy note; the iris, or parson-bird, who wears a glossy black suit; and the New Zealand robin, who is not a robin at all, but has a yellowy-white breast. Then there is a very troublesome little bird called a weka, or wood-hen, which runs like a weasel, which the natives eat. These are very bold little fellows; they come into the farm-yards of the settlers and suck the hens' eggs. One of these disturbed Lady Barker when she was lying half-asleep, by giving her a sudden dig in her arm with its beak.

The strangest bird in New Zealand is the kiwi, or apteryx, of which there are three or four species. These have no wings or tails, and are covered with hair. They are only about the size of an ordinary fowl, but they are the representatives of a wonderful race of birds which once lived in New Zealand, which the natives call moas, of which perfect skeletons have been found in various parts of the islands. Some of these are as much as fifteen feet high. An egg was once found in a native grave ten inches long and seven broad. The Maories say that their ancestors used to hunt these wonderful wingless birds for food. There are complete skeletons of moas to be seen in the South Kensington Museum.

The Maories are tall, well-built men, almost equal to Englishmen in weight and strength. Their hair is black and coarse, but not woolly like a negro's; and they have large noses and mouths. They tattoo their faces most elegantly and elaborately, though I believe in these days the young men are giving up the custom a good deal, but the women, who are not, generally speaking, so nice-looking as the men, would still be considered

MAORI CHIEF AND WIFE.

very unattractive unless their under lips were adorned in this manner.

The process of tattooing, as practised by the natives, is most painful and tedious. A preparation of charcoal is made and placed on a block of wood. Then incisions are made in the skin with a bone instrument dipped in the charcoal. The finer part of the work is finished up with a bone needle, more after the fashion in which our sailors' tattoo their arms with gunpowder. It used to be the universal custom to begin tattooing a wretched Maori boy at the age of ten, and continue the process at intervals till he was twenty. Many years ago a party of Englishmen were seized and tattooed by the Maories. One of them (a Mr. Rutherford) gives a terrible account of the suffering entailed by it. He was held

TATTOOING A CHIEF.

down by six natives, and the operation lasted for four hours. The Maories themselves, however, do not seem to mind the pain of it, and tattoo their own persons, as well as those of their friends, with the greatest satisfaction. The tattooing of the face of a New Zealander marks the clan or tribe to which he belongs, like the stripes and colour of a Highlander's plaid. Besides these distinguishing lines and curves, the intricacies and varieties of the pattern are like a crest or coat-of-arms, and mark the Maori chiefs from the common people, and also enable them to distinguish their enemies in battle.

Besides the tattooing, they smear their faces with oil and red ochre, which is considered highly ornamental. One of the early missionaries to the South Sea Islands, a Mr. Ellis, who stayed for a short time in New Zealand on his way, mentions that the only inconvenience he experienced during his visit was from this oil and red ochre, which, in spite of all his efforts, would adhere to his clothes, particularly after saluting the Maories in their own peculiar fashion by rubbing noses!

The Maories have many superstitions, some of which are most curious and others very silly and childish. One of the strongest is the " tapu," which means that a thing is sacred—not to be touched. The first missionaries and other Europeans often got into trouble by transgressing these laws unintentionally, and sometimes the Maories would lay traps for them, as it were, putting the sacred object in their way so as to give them an excuse for killing or injuring them. The chiefs are always tapu, especially their heads. Many places are tapu; birds and animals are sometimes tapu. In these days, however, the tapu is not nearly so strict

as it used to be; the Maories will often take it off for
money. When the Duke of Edinburgh reached the hot
lakes in the North Island, the tapu was taken off the
very sacred ducks which abound there, for his benefit; so
that in such a case as this it really only amounts to a
useful preservation of game.

A stranger custom than the tapu is what is called
" muru." If any one has an accident or affliction, it is
thought a compliment and a token of sympathy to visit
him, eat up all his provisions, and sometimes rob him of
everything he possesses.

There is a very amusing old book called the
" Pakeha Maori" (Pakeha means a stranger), which
describes this custom of " muru" fully. " A man's
child fell into the fire and was nearly burned to death.
The father was immediately plundered to an extent that
almost left him without the means of subsistence—
fishing-nets, canoes, pigs, provisions, all went. His
canoe upset, and he and all his family narrowly escaped
drowning; some were perhaps drowned. He was immediately robbed, and well pummelled with a club into
the bargain. He might be clearing some land for
potatoes, burning off the fern, and the fire spreads
farther than he intended, and gets into the ' wahi tapu,'
or burial-ground. No matter whether anyone has been
buried in it for the last hundred years, he is tremendously
robbed. In fact, for ten thousand different causes a
man might be robbed. . . . Indeed, in many cases it
would have been felt as a slight and an insult not to be
robbed—the sacking of a man's establishment being
often taken as a high compliment—and to resist the
execution would not only have been looked upon as mean
and disgraceful in the highest degree, but would have

A MAORI CARVED MONUMENT.

debarred the contemptible individual from the privilege of robbing his neighbour."

There were many worse superstitions and customs than these, however, against which the missionaries had to contend when they first took up their abode among the Maories. When a chief died, it was considered right and proper to kill a slave immediately, in order that the great man might have a spirit to attend him into another world. A daughter of Mr. Marsden, the first missionary to New Zealand, describes how, on one occasion, during her father's absence, a young New Zealander died, the nephew of a chief, who was staying at his house in Sydney. The uncle chief immediately prepared to sacrifice a slave, to accompany the spirit of his nephew, and Mr. Marsden's family were only able to save the life of the poor fellow by hiding him. When Mr. Marsden came home, he persuaded the chieftain with great difficulty to give up the idea; but he was never thoroughly satisfied about it. He frequently lamented that his nephew had no attendant to the next world, and seemed quite afraid to return to New Zealand lest the father of the young man should reproach him with his neglect.

When a chieftain died, one or more of his wives would always make an end to herself, in order that she might accompany her husband. In these days the wives content themselves with covering their heads, and howling and lamenting for days together. These lamentations and certain ceremonies and a great deal of feasting always accompany the death of a chief, and constitute what they call a "tangi"—one of the most curious of New Zealand customs.

The Maories often erect beautiful carved monuments

to the memory of their chiefs.    Sometimes the carvings
are very grotesque.    One was described to me which
was covered with strange figures, with men's faces and
enormous eyes made of mother-of-pearl.

TATTOOED NEW ZEALANDER.

# CHAPTER II.

## MISSION LIFE AMONG THE MAORIES.

Missionary Work—Bishop Patteson—Mr. Marsden and Ruatara—Early Converts.

THERE are no men in the world of whom we ought to think more kindly and more respectfully than missionaries, and yet, strange to say, in all parts of the world we meet people inclined to laugh at or find fault with their efforts.

Nothing can be more wrong and foolish than this spirit, but it often arises from mere ignorance or want of thought. Those who talk so lightly and disparagingly of missionaries and their work do not stop to consider the hardships and sacrifices of their lives—how they have left their native land, many, if not all, of those most dear to them, and all their home-comforts, associations, and friends, to carry out, according to their lights, our Lord's command to preach the Gospel in all lands. They brave every sort of discomfort, privation, and pestilential climate. They are often lonely, often misunderstood. Sometimes, like other people, they make mistakes; sometimes they lay down their lives at the hands of those very heathen for whom they have sacrificed so much. They may seem to us quite unsuccessful in what they have tried to do, and we may think their lives thrown away; but of this we, with our short human sight, cannot really judge. The good seed they have sown may spring up at any time, though neither they nor we may ever see the fruit, and the Master whom they served will not judge their work as we do in this world, by the amount of their success here. Of each good and faithful servant He will assuredly say, "He hath done what he could."

And there are others besides the missionaries who have a share in their work, whom we should not forget, who claim our warmest sympathy and admiration. They are the families and near relations of the missionaries, who, like the father and sisters of the good Bishop Patteson, cheerfully give up their best and dearest, and let him go forth, knowing that they may never see him again in this world, to carry God's message of love to those who would never otherwise hear it. No one, I think, can read the account of Coleridge Patteson's life in his happy Devonshire curacy, and how when Bishop Selwyn, "who had long been the subject of his deep and silent enthusiasm," came to England, and he resolved if possible to return with him to New Zealand, the old widowed father, who adored him, at once agreed to give him up, without feeling that his share in the sacrifice was almost as great as that of his son. In one of her first letters to her brother, Miss Fanny Patteson writes, "Dear Coley, it is very hard to live without you;" and he says in answer that he read on in her letter till he came to this passage, and that then he broke down and cried like a child. "I was quite alone," he writes from Auckland, "out in the fields on a glorious bright day, and it was the relief I had longed for. The few simple words told me the whole story, and I prayed with my whole heart that you might find strength in the hour of sadness." And then he goes on to advise her how best to bear her grief, not by driving away the thought of the separation, but by dwelling on it calmly, and trying to find spiritual help and comfort in it. He seems to have realised the grief his absence was causing his family most vividly, and to feel that their sacrifice in parting with him made them fully sharers in his work. In the same letter to his sister, he writes :—

"There is One above who knows what a trial it is to you. For myself, hard as it is—almost too hard sometimes—yet I have relief in the variety and unceasing multiplicity of my occupations. Not a moment of any day can I be said to be idle. But for you, with more time for meditating, with no change of scene, with every object that meets you at home and in your daily walks reminding you of me, it must indeed be such a trial as angels love to look upon when it is borne patiently, and with a perfect assurance that God is ordering all things for our good; and so let us struggle on to the end. All good powers are on our side, and we shall meet, by the infinite mercy, one day, when there shall be no separation for ever."

The history of the early labours of the missionaries
in New Zealand, the forerunners of the good Bishops
Selwyn and Patteson, are very interesting and wonderful.   Those who first went there, and settled among the
Maories at the time when their frightful cannibalism
prevailed, must have been indeed brave as well as good
men.   No motive but pure love to Christ and their fellow-

BISHOP COLERIDGE PATTESON.

creatures could have been strong enough to induce people
to risk their lives in a country in this respect so horribly
savage, and it was the missionaries who first paved the
way for the settlers, who came so fast later on, and made
happy homes for themselves and their families in the
beautiful island, with its fertile soil and delightful
climate.

The first missionary who ventured to take up his abode among the Maories was the Rev. Samuel Marsden, whose name is still remembered there with the utmost

MISSION STATION AT WANGANUI, NEW ZEALAND.

love and respect. He was chaplain to the convict settlement at that time in New South Wales, and the accounts which reached him there of the New Zealanders, of their intelligence and many noble qualities on the one hand, and their frightful cruelty on the other, filled him with a longing desire to preach the Gospel to them and

o

show them a better way of life. In 1808 he visited England, and at that time laid the foundation of the Church of England mission in New Zealand. The story of the young Maori cheiftain, Ruatara, who was Mr. Marsden's friend and assistant from the very beginning, is so interesting that I must tell it you here. Some years before Mr. Marsden went to New Zealand, Ruatara (the name means a lizard), seized with a longing desire to see something of the lands where the white men came from, embarked in an European whaling ship which had put into the New Zealand port called the "Bay of Islands." He worked his way as a common sailor in that and other vessels, generally speaking, I am sorry to say, treated most roughly and unkindly by those about him. One captain only, of the name of Richardson, appears to have been kind to him and paid him properly for his services. His great desire was to get to England and to see the chief of the wonderful people there, and at length the captain of a ship called the *Santa Anna* offered to take him to England, promising him a sight of King George on his arrival, and he willingly risked the voyage for the sake of the reward at the end.

When they arrived in England he claimed the promise, but the captain was faithless; sometimes he was told that no one was allowed to see King George, sometimes that his house could not be found, so that he was continually disappointed. He was scarcely allowed to go on shore at all, and saw hardly anything of London, and in about a fortnight was put on board the *Ann*, a convict ship bound for Australia. At that very time Mr. Marsden was in London, busy with arrangements for the mission to New Zealand, in which he had succeeded in interesting many good people, and little thinking that a young Maori chief was so near him and in such miserable circumstances. It was in the *Ann* that Mr. Marsden and his fellow-labourers embarked, bound for Australia, on their way to New Zealand. When he had been at sea for a few days, he observed a dark-skinned man wrapped in an old great coat, who seemed to be suffering terribly from the cold, and who appeared as if in almost the last stage of consumption. This was poor Ruatara, who had fallen very ill from cold and misery, and who poured forth his adventures and injuries into Mr. Marsden's kind sympathising ears. It is very piteous to think of the state of this poor fellow, who had believed in the white man, and had left his native land and sunny climate, and had endured so much hardship and suffering, only to be ill-treated and cheated. From that time, however, he received every attention and kindness from Mr. Marsden and his friends, and as they got into warmer latitudes recovered his health.

When they arrived in Australia, Mr. Marsden took Ruatara with him to his own house, where he remained with him for some months, learning from him how to cultivate corn and vegetables, and listening with great interest to the first truths of Christianity which Mr. Marsden taught him, though he was very slow in unstanding them. There were other young New Zealand chiefs who had been fired, like Ruatara, with a longing to travel and visit other countries; but all had not his patient, forgiving disposition. One of them, known by the name of "George," had also embarked in an English ship and had been cruelly treated, and took a terrible revenge. On the return of the vessel to New Zealand, he persuaded the captain to land on a part of the island where his own tribe lived, promising him wood, and

c 2

water, and everything he wanted. The captain and a large party went on shore, and at George's instigation the natives surrounded them and soon overpowered and killed them, after which they took their clothes, and went off to the ship in the boats and murdered all on board. The news of this dreadful attack on the English by the Maories reached Sydney soon after the arrival of Mr. Marsden's party, and in consequence it was not thought safe for the missionaries to proceed to New Zealand for some years later. They employed the time in studying the Maori language, and making friends with individual native chiefs who were invited over to visit them.

After further adventures at sea, and another visit to Mr. Marsden, Ruatara returned to his native country, after an absence of seven years, well supplied by his English friends with tools and plants and seeds of various kinds, to introduce in his own country. He was most warmly received by his relations, but, to his great disappointment, they declined to believe his wonderful stories of the things he had seen. Nothing would persuade them to believe that the bread and biscuits they had seen in the ships could be made from the grains of wheat he showed them. When, in attempting to describe the horses, he called them "corraddees," (their native name for a dog) large enough and willing to carry a man, they were most indignant. A few, however, at once proceeded to test the possibility of animals being used to carry men by attempting to ride their pigs. Naturally the conduct of the pigs during the experiment was not such as to convince them of Ruatara's truthfulness. With some difficulty he persuaded six of the chiefs to accept some of his wheat, and sow it in the ground according to his directions. It came up well,

A MAORI CHIEF (UNTATTOOED).

but just as it was coming into ear he found it all destroyed. The Maories could not understand any mode
of growth different to their own kumera, or sweet potato,
and had examined the roots, hoping to find young grain
round them potato-fashion. When they found nothing
they considered the whole thing a failure, and pulled up
the plants and burned them. Only one among them—an
uncle of Ruatara's, called "Hongi"—had patience to wait
till the wheat was full-grown, and he and his nephew
were rewarded by plentiful crops, to the great astonishment of every one. Their fields were reaped and the corn
threshed, and then poor Ruatara found he could go no
further, for he had no mill to grind it in. He tried to use
a coffee-mill, which he borrowed from a tradingship, but
without any success, and was only laughed at for his pains.

While Ruatara was thus trying to improve the condition of his countrymen, without much encouragement,
Mr. Marsden, in New South Wales, was busy preparing
the way for his great missionary enterprise. He was never
daunted by delays and difficulties; he knew he must bide
his time till the right moment should come. The
Church Missionary Society furnished him with a small
ship called the *Active* for his purposes, and in this
he sent two of his party, Mr. King and Mr. Hall, taking
with them the present of a hand-mill, for grinding corn.
Nothing could have been more acceptable. Ruatara had
at length the delight of convincing his friends of the
truth of his stories. They assembled in large numbers
to watch the experiment, and when a little cake was
produced, hastily baked in a frying-pan, their delight
knew no bounds; they danced about and shouted with
joy. Now they really began to believe Ruatara when
he told them that the missionaries were good and trust-

worthy men; and so the way was paved for Mr. Marsden's mission. On the 19th of November, 1814, he embarked in the *Active*, with about thirty-five people —three missionaries besides himself, with their wives and children, eight New Zealanders, including Ruatara and his uncle, Hongi, a great warrior chief, two Otaheitans, the master of the ship and his wife and son, and four Europeans belonging to the ship, two sawyers, one smith, and a runaway convict they found on board, one bull, two cows, and a few sheep and poultry. Mr. Marsden's journal and letters to England, in which he gives an account of his arrival in New Zealand, are most interesting even now, and we can imagine with what deep anxiety and interest they were read at the time by his friends and relations, and all the members and well-wishers of the Church Missionary Society. The *Active* anchored near the Bay of Islands, at the very spot where the dreadful massacre had taken place. The chiefs went on shore first, and a friendly communication was at once opened with the natives, who had sent a canoe to the ship with some fish before the chiefs had landed. Still, however friendly they might seem, it must have required great faith and courage for the missionaries to land on these wild shores, feeling how entirely they were at the mercy of the tribe who had so ruthlessly murdered and devoured their countrymen. There was a frightful war raging at that very time between two Maori tribes, and Mr. Marsden was determined, if possible, to be the means of making peace between them. Ruatara tried to dissuade him from making the attempt; but finding that he was determined to try, he accompanied the party on shore, and made the first advance. They had no sooner landed than they

A MAORI FESTIVAL.

saw a body of armed men stationed on the hill. Ruatara went forward, and explained that some white men desired to visit them. The pause that followed must have been a terribly anxious one for the missionaries. Suddenly a woman came running towards them, waving a red mat over her head, and calling out "Haromai, haromai!" "Come hither, come hither!"

This, they were assured, was a friendly invitation. So they went forward, and soon found themselves in the midst of warriors and spears. Suddenly the warriors seized their spears, brandished them in the air, uttered the most frightful shrieks and yells, and flung their limbs and bodies about in the most horrible manner. This was, however, really only a compliment to the visitors, and was, in fact, a war dance of *welcome*. This method of showing pleasure at the presence of guests seems very strange, but other customs of the Maories are no less so. As an instance, the following account of a festival may be given:—At a time of great rejoicing the Maories erected a huge platform eighty or ninety feet high, in the shape of a pyramid, as shown in the illustration. The whole of the structure was covered with people, who literally swarmed upon it, and assisted in decorating it with coloured cloths and streamers, and such ornaments as they could afford.

But to return to the missionaries. As evening drew on, all the party returned to the ship except Mr. Marsden and his friend, Mr. Nicholas, who determined to remain, and, if possible, carry out their plan. They had supper of fish and potatoes in one camp, and then walked to the hostile one, about a mile off, where they were received quite as kindly, and were soon surrounded by chiefs. Mr. Marsden then addressed them, George, who spoke English well, acting as interpreter. He explained the object of the missionaries in coming to live among them ; and showed how much peace would conduce in every way to the welfare of all parties. The first night passed among the natives must have been indeed a strange one. Mr. Marsden describes it in this way :—"As the evening advanced, the people began to retire to rest in different groups. About eleven o'clock Mr. Nicholas and I wrapped ourselves in our great coats, and prepared for rest. George directed me to lie by his side. His wife and child lay on the right hand, and Mr. Nicholas close by. The night was clear, the stars shone bright, and the sea in our front was smooth ; around us were innumerable spears, stuck upright in the ground, and groups of natives lying in all directions, like a flock of sheep, upon the grass, as there were neither tents nor huts to cover them. I viewed our present situation with sensations that I cannot express, surrounded by cannibals who had massacred and devoured our countrymen. I wondered much at the mysteries of providence, and how these things could be. Never did I behold the blessed advantage of civilisation in a more grateful light than now. I did not sleep much during the night. My mind was too seriously occupied by the present scene, and the new and strange ideas it naturally excited. About three in the morning I rose and walked about the camp, surveying the different groups of natives. When the morning light returned, we beheld men, women, and children asleep in all directions, like the beasts of the field." The next morning the chiefs were invited to breakfast on board the *Active*. Mr. Marsden was a little afraid that they would not dare to put themselves in the power of the white men, for fear

they might revenge themselves on them for their former
outrage ; but they accepted the invitation quite readily,
which shows how Mr. Marsden must have already
succeeded in inspiring them with confidence. After
breakfast, all the presents the missionaries had brought
with them—axes, bill-hooks, prints—the men got ready,
and the chiefs were all seated in the cabin with great
formality. Ruatara stood and handed each article
separately to Mr. Marsden, to give the visitors, who
were greatly delighted. Mr. Marsden then explained
to them how Mr. Hanson, who commanded the *Active*,
would be employed in bringing axes and all the things
that were wanted to enable them to cultivate and improve their country, from Sydney. He then expressed a
hope that from that time they would have no more
wars, but live in peace together, and had the great
pleasure and satisfaction of seeing the hostile chiefs
rubbing each other's noses in token of reconciliation.

Some of the presents astonished the New Zealanders
immensely, especially the cows and horses, which they
had never seen, nor, indeed, believed in, and poor
Ruatara had once more the satisfaction of proving the
truth of his stories. The sight of Mr. Marsden really
mounted on a horse caused infinite amazement.

Ruatara took the greatest delight in introducing and
making welcome his English friends, and showed them
with much pride the crops he had raised from the seed
they had given him. Here, among his own people, he
was a great man, and he used his influence for the benefit
of the white strangers in every possible way. The
second day after their arrival was a Sunday, and also
Christmas Day, which we must remember means the
height of summer on that side of the world; and when

Mr. Marsden came on deck, the cheering sight met him of the Union Jack flying, hoisted on a flagstaff by the faithful Ruatara in honour of the holy day. He had been early at work, in preparation for the first divine worship ever held in New Zealand since the creation. He had enclosed some land within a fence, and made a pulpit and reading-desk in the middle; these he covered with some cloth he had brought from

MAORI WAR DANCE

Australia. Then he arranged some old canoes for seats. All went on shore for the service. The English were placed on the canoe-seats, on each side of the pulpit, and Ruatara and two other chiefs, dressed in uniforms given them by the Governor, stood in the enclosure with their men round them, with swords by their sides and switches in their hands. The inhabitants of the town, with the women and children and other chiefs, formed a circle round the whole; all assembled to hear for the first time "the glad tidings of great joy" which Mr. Marsden brought them. One cannot imagine a more solemn or impressive scene. No wonder that

GETTING EXCITED.

Mr. Marsden writes, "I rose up and began the service with singing the old Hundredth Psalm; and felt my very soul melt within me when I viewed my congregation and considered the state they were in. After reading the service, during which the natives stood up and sat down at the signals given by Koro Koro's switch, which was regulated by the movements of the Europeans, it being Christmas Day, I preached from the second chapter of St Luke's Gospel and tenth verse: 'Behold, I bring you glad tidings of great joy,' &c. The natives told Ruatara that they could not understand what I meant. He replied that they were not to mind that now, for they would understand by-and-bye, and that he would explain my meaning as far as he could. When I had done preaching, he informed them what I had been talking about. . . . In this manner the Gospel has been introduced into New Zealand; and I fervently pray that the glory of it may never depart from its inhabitants till time shall be no more."

# CHAPTER III.

## MISSION WORK AMONG THE MAORIES.

Difficulties in the Way—Maori Massacres
—Mr. and Mrs. Williams—The First
Baptism.

THUS bravely and hopefully Mr. Samuel Marsden started on his great work; but there were terrible and anxious times in store for the missionaries before their object could be at all accomplished. The Maories were more anxious to get hold of all the useful articles the missionaries brought than to listen to their preaching. "If we believe will you give us blankets?" they used to say; and it was very hard to tell when they had really and truly received into their hearts the Gospel tidings.

Not long after Mr. Marsden's arrival Ruatara died, and the loss of his protection and friendship was a grievous one. His uncle, Hongi, the great warrior, was kind to the missionaries in the main, but there was a time when his whole soul became absorbed in the desire to obtain European arms and ammunition, and this led him to countenance many bad actions. Ruatara's great object had been to improve and raise his fellow countrymen, but Hongi cared more for his own personal glory. Mr. Marsden could not remain permanently in New Zealand ; he left the other missionaries there, and went backwards and forwards between it and Australia every few years, always bringing fresh hope and encouragement with him.

The history of the anxieties and sufferings of the missionaries during their first years is very sad, and very wonderful, to read. At first they had only huts made of flags and rushes to live in, and the wind and the rain came in, and the floor was often deep in mud. When they were able to build better houses and cultivate the land they had bought, and collect comfortable things about them, the natives would constantly invade their premises, with or without excuses, and ask for or take anything they fancied. Their stores of blankets, flour, clothing, etc., were frequently robbed, and their poultry seized and killed before their eyes. Often their property was injured out of mere mischief. The natives would break down their fences, let their cattle loose into the bush, and drive their pigs into the wheat. Sometimes these attacks would be accompanied by frightful threats, such as that the stones of the oven in which they were to be cooked were then heating ; and often they were left almost destitute of food and clothing.

The wives of the missionaries worked and bore their discomforts and privations as bravely as their husbands. They could get little help in their household work, as the

native girls were most capricious and exacting as to the
kind of payment they expected. Worse than all were
the terrible scenes of savage warfare continually going
on round them, which they had no power to stop, and
could only protest against, and the knowledge of the
horrible cannibalism which took place after every battle.

Mr. Marsden writes: "I have met with no family
but some branches of it had been killed in battle and
afterwards eaten. If any chief falls into the hands of a
tribe which he has oppressed and injured, by the chances
of war, they are sure to roast and eat him, and preserve
his bones in the family as a memento of his fate, and
convert them into fish-hooks, whistles, and ornaments."

Through all these horrors and miseries the missionaries went calmly on their way, never losing sight for a
moment of their high calling, as those who were bringing light to a dark land, though at first it burned so
dim and feebly. They never seem, to judge by their
letters and journals, to have been troubled with fears for
the safety of their own lives, though they must have
carried them, as it were, in their hands. It was only
long afterwards that they seemed to have realised their
danger fully. Twenty years later, Mr. King said that
he could not then look back to those days without
shuddering.

Mr. Marsden's second visit to New Zealand brought,
as ever, help and comfort, and the missionary settlement
was now established in the Bay of Islands, at a beautiful
spot on the banks of the " Keri-keri," near a waterfall,
which the natives called " Rainbow Water."

Hongi was chieftain in this part of the country, and
he was most anxious that the missionaries should settle
there. It was a few years after this that he visited

D

England, having a great desire to see the King and
his people, and know what they were doing. The
missionaries were delighted at the idea of his going, as
they thought naturally that he would be able better to
help them and understand them when he had seen
their country. He was treated very differently to poor
Ruatara on his visit. He received every attention and
kindness from the friends to the mission and to the
civilisation of New Zealand, and the interview with
King George, which Ruatara had longed for in vain,
was achieved; but unhappily he returned to his native
country with his newly-acquired weapons of destruction,
presented to him by the King, bent only on using them
to subdue other tribes, and increase his own importance
and power. After this there were most terrible wars in
the country round the Bay of Islands; Hongi and his
men attacked neighbouring tribes, who had no chance
against the European weapons. For a time the missionaries were left nearly alone, for all the men were obliged
to accompany him, and he took even the children with
him, saying he wished them to learn to fight and not to
read. Villages were burned, and hundreds of prisoners
killed and eaten, and horrors of every kind committed;
but through all the missionaries clung to their posts,
and hoped and prayed when they could do nothing else.

About this time their hands and hearts were
strengthened by the arrival of a new helper, Mr. Henry
Williams, another English clergyman, who, with his wife,
accompanied Mr. Marsden on one of his periodical visits.
Of the many different histories of the missions to New
Zealand which have been written, none is more interesting than the life of Mr. Williams. Of all that good
and brave band, no one seems to have understood the

Maori character so well as he, to have entered so fully and
entirely into their feelings, and to have gained their confidence so
completely;
but    this
was    the
work   of
years  of
toil,  and
patience, and devotion.   For forty-four
years Mr. Williams was a missionary
in New Zealand.

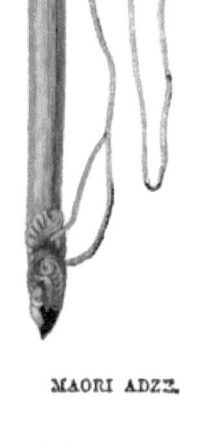

MAORI ADZE.

His earliest longings were for a
seafaring life.  Mr. Carleton, who has
written the story of his life so carefully, and with such true reverence and
appreciation, tells us that from the
time he was able to think for himself
he had made up his mind to be a sailor
and nothing else, like his grandfather
and three uncles.   When quite a child
he made a model of a man-of-war,
with rigging and sails complete, only
from a description in the Encyclopædia.
He went into the navy when fourteen
years old, and served there many years,
taking part in several important en-
gagements, and gaining experience of
various kinds, which was, no doubt,
most useful to him in the latter part of
his career.  His first thought of becoming a missionary came to him in a
very simple way.  He was in the habit of taking in a

D 2

single periodical, the *Naval Chronicle*. His brother-in-law persuaded him to take in also the *Missionary Register*. There he read how the people of Tahiti had burned their idols, and learned to know the true God, and he resolved, says Mr. Carleton, "to embark in the service of Christ, and consecrate the rest of his days to those wild and dangerous islands, which were then the subject of romance, of curiosity, and of dread." The account of the building and launching of the first New Zealand ship, under the sailor-missionary's superintendence, is most interesting. The labour of this great work must have been immense, but to Mr. Williams it was a labour of love. The whole undertaking, from the felling the timber, and rolling the logs into the river, to the final launching of the vessel, had to be conducted under his own eye; he was obliged to manage and direct the native sawyers and carpenters—no easy task—and often worked away himself with adze and auger. Of course, the only native experience in such matters lay in the building their own canoes, for which purpose they have very peculiar instruments of their own manufacture, with which they scoop out the wood. Their war-canoes are very strong and well made, and sometimes as much as eighty feet long.

The natives took a deep interest in the building of Mr. Williams' little ship, though they appear to have given him a good deal of trouble during the process. It was named the *Herald*, and the day it was launched must have been a proud and happy one for Mr. Williams. The missionaries had long been sorely in need of such a possession, not only to fetch them all sorts of things they were in want of, but to enable them to visit the southern islands. Here is the

account of the great day, as given in Mr. Williams'
life :—

"The launch of the *Herald* was, to the natives, a
sensational event.   Due notice had been given ; a fleet
of boats and canoes had assembled; numbers had come
from inland, partly from curiosity, partly in hope of
payment; upon a rough estimate, from three to four
thousand persons were present.   Mr. Williams had been
out the night before inspecting the ways, and taking
every precaution against any risk of failure.   The
natives, who had supposed that the vessel was to be
moved off in Maori style, by main force, had passed
their time in calculating the amount of payment they
were to receive, and in devising pretexts for extortion.
As was the difference in size between a canoe and a
fifty-ton vessel, so was to be the difference of payment
for service.   They declared that they would not move a
hand till their terms should have been complied with,
enforcing the demand by divers weighty and ingenious
reasons, in reply to each of which they got nothing but
a quiet nod of the head.   They were already engaged,
by anticipation, in apportioning the payment among
themselves, when Mr. Williams announced that all was
ready.   But instead of going among the mob to clench
a bargain, he walked up to the vessel and named her.
This was the signal for the start.   The dog-shores were
knocked away; the ship glided gently down the ways
into the water, to the utter amazement of the natives,
who rose as one man with a roar of 'Ana na, ana
na-a-a-a.'   The young men, rushing after her into the
water, throwing their spears at her as she glided along,
swam off and clambered up her sides; others, crouching on
their knees at the water's edge, made hideous faces,

thrusting out their tongues and rolling their eyes as
they would to the enemy before battle.  The Europeans
gave three hearty cheers; the natives on shore broke
out into a furious war dance, which was answered by
those on board, to the no small risk of upsetting the
light craft, as she lay, unballasted, high out of the water.

"As the vessel was getting into deep water she
touched upon a sand-bank, and stuck fast for a few
minutes.  A line was carried out to moorings which
had been laid for the purpose, the end being brought on
shore to haul upon.  No demur, no talk of payment
now; the natives rushed down with one accord, bent on
to the line, and easily had her over the bank.  All
seemed delighted, Europeans and Maories vieing with
each other in congratulation at the success of the
launch.  The natives were intensely gratified and
amazed, deeming themselves amply rewarded by having
witnessed the wonderful genius of the 'pakeha,' who by
only knocking away a wedge could launch such a huge
canoe."

Mrs. Williams' early letters, after her own and her
husband's arrival in New Zealand, are very interesting,
and amusing as well.  Her bright, cheerful spirit never
seems to have failed her.  She was most kindly welcomed by the natives when she landed at the new
mission station, Paihia.  They crowded round and held
out their hands to her, calling out, "The wife ! Give me
your hand !"  Mrs. Williams writes with delight of
her new home, a raupo hut, which, she says, looked like
a bee-hive, except in shape, with its garden and corn-
fields; but her domestic troubles seem to have been
great.  The native girls whom she got to help her
could not be trusted alone for a moment to do the

household work, and if the day was hot would run off
to the river for a swim, or lie down and go to sleep for
two or three hours. If she found fault with them they
would tell her she had "too much of the mouth."

The natives, though kindly disposed on the whole
towards Mr. Williams and his family, were inclined to
take liberties, and more substantial articles. On
these occasions Mr. Williams always treated them with
the utmost firmness and coolness, never showing the
slightest fear of them. The only way in which he could
punish these offences was to *tuhi-tuhi* the offender—
that is, note him down in writing, and refuse to speak
to or shake hands with him. This the natives always
felt very much.

Sometimes the chief would take Mr. Williams' part,
when he reported these things to him, and insist on
restitution being made. Mrs. Williams gives a most
amusing account—though she must have been far too
frightened to be amused at the time—of the behaviour of
a chief called "Tohipatu," who lived about a mile off.
Instead of knocking at the gate for admittance, he
suddenly sprang over the fence round Mr. Williams'
house. A gentleman called Mr. Fairburn, who was
present, told him that he was a bad man for coming in
like a thief and not like a gentleman. On this he
began to stamp and caper about like a madman, brandishing his spear and springing like a cat at Mr. Fairburn.
Mr. Williams now came up, and told him he was
behaving very badly, but he continued to spring about
and flourish the green-stone weapon, called a *meré*, which
every chief carries concealed under his mat. Mr.
Williams and Mr. Fairburn then left him and went
down to the beach, and he went also, but soon returned

with a long pole, with which he struck at the gate; but as it did not yield to the stroke, he jumped over the

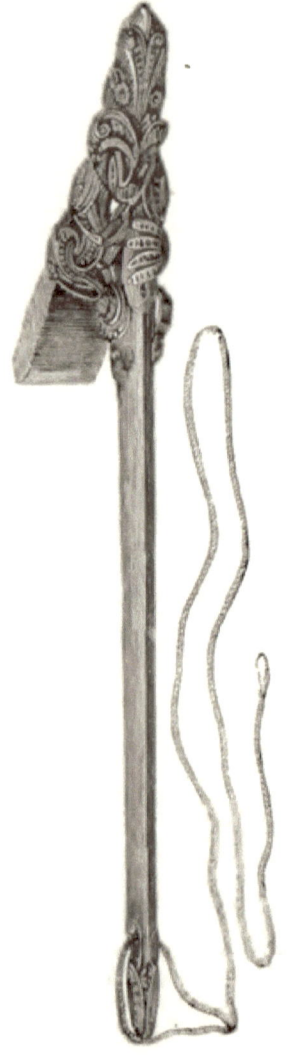

MAORI ADZE.

fence again, and resumed all his old anties, and when Mr. Williams returned, couched and aimed his spear at him again. He said he had hurt his foot in jumping over the fence, and must have payment for it. Mr. Williams told him it was well that he had hurt his foot when he had come in such a manner, and that he should have no payment. He then walked to an outhouse, where various useful things were kept, and seized an old iron pot in which pitch had been boiled, and tried to leap the fence with it; but Mr. Williams darted on him, snatched the pot out of his hands, and set his own back against the door, calling to some one to take the pot. Poor Mrs. Williams looked out of the window and saw her husband standing there with his arms folded, and looking as if he were keeping a savage bull at bay, while Tohi sprang about in an indescribable manner, stamping and making horrid gestures, and then squatting down and panting, as if trying to work himself up to make the fatal spring. He said he should stay there "to-

day and to-morrow, and five days more, and make a
great fight, and to-morrow ten and ten and ten men
(holding up his fingers as he spoke) would come and
set fire to the house." During evening prayers he was
more quiet, and sat by the fire at the back of the house,
but after prayers he came back, with his wife and some
more natives, to the window of the room where Mr.
Williams and his family sat, and, without ceremony,
put in his leg, and, pointing to his foot, demanded payment for the injury. Mr. Williams told him to go away
and come to-morrow like a gentleman, and knock at the
gate, as Te Haki, another chief, did, and then he would
say, "How do you do, Mr. Tohitapu?" and invite him
to breakfast. On this he declared his foot was too bad to
walk, and then sprang about more wildly than ever. It
was now eleven o'clock at night. Poor Mrs. Williams sat
down and tried to write, and the friendly natives looking
in at the window kept saying, "Mother, you see a great
fire in the house. Oh, yes! children dead, all dead, a
great fight, a great many men, plenty of muskets!"
which must have been anything but comforting to her.
At length they ventured to go to bed, and the friendly
chiefs wrapped themselves in their blankets, and slept on
the ground, one keeping watch. Early in the morning
they were wakened by a great noise made by Tohi and
others; but Mrs. Williams quietly got up and made
breakfast as usual, handing tea out to her friends. She
sent a pint pot of tea to Tohi, hoping it might soothe
him; but he drank it off and continued as wild as ever,
prancing about in the yard with his followers, hideous
figures armed with spears and hatchets and a few
muskets.

It must have been dreadful for poor Mrs. Williams

to look out, knowing her husband was in the midst, exposed to such danger, and she had to remain shut up with her children, the windows blocked with native heads looking in. About five o'clock Mr. Williams came up to the window, and said things were quieter now, and the natives dispersed; and as the poor children were pining for fresh air, Mrs. Williams put them out through the window. At that moment there was a tremendous noise. Mr. Williams put back the children head foremost, and ran off. A chief brought back the little boy, who must have wandered a short distance off, screaming. Mrs. Williams asked if he was hurt, and the poor child answered :—"No, mamma, I am not hurt, but they are going to kill papa. We shall all be burned, and they will kill poor papa. I saw the men; I saw the guns."

It must have been a terrible moment for poor Mrs. Williams, as she sat there waiting, with the baby in her arms, and the other three children crying and clinging to her. They all knelt down and repeated a prayer after her for the safety of their father, and presently the noise ceased, and a good-natured native woman put her head in at the window and told Mrs. Williams that there would be no more fight that day. Soon she had the happiness of unbolting the door to let in her husband, who told her all was over, and that Tohitapu had gone off quietly with the iron pot, which had been presented to him as a peace-offering.

Soon after Mr. Williams's arrival the first native baptism took place. It was so hard to be sure that the Gospel they preached was really understood and accepted, even by those natives who professed to be converted, that the missionaries were very slow to baptise a Maori,

and it was more than ten years after the beginning of
the Mission before they felt justified in doing so. The
old chief Rangi was baptised on his death-bed by the
name of Christian, surrounded by his countrymen, who
seemed greatly interested and impressed. "To us,"
Mr. Williams writes, "it was a season of joy and gladness, a period to which I had been looking with great
interest." His description of the old chief, and how he
spoke to those around him of the darkness that had once
encompassed his soul, and his sure and certain hope in
dying, is very remarkable.

In the missionaries' letters we find frequent
mention of individual natives who seemed specially
drawn to them and their teachings. We hear of the
great fighting chief Jaiwanga, who had spent all his
time in the most savage warfare, building a hut like the
English, and settling down to a quiet country life. He
became so fond of his garden, which was full of vegetables, vines, melons, and peaches, that at last nothing
would induce him to leave it to join the wars. Then we
hear of Dudi Dudi, a young slave, who was very slow
in being converted from his superstition, but who prayed
constantly for light, which dawned on him quite
suddenly, when he was filled with peace and joy; of a
girl named Peti, who died of consumption, bearing her
sufferings with the utmost patience, and saying
beautiful things to those around her; and of many
others.

There was an old chief of the name of Akaipikia,
whom the Bishop of Waipu describes in his interesting
book, "Christianity among the New Zealanders," who
had lost the use of his limbs through eating the
poisonous berries of the karaka-tree. Once when one of

the missionaries visited him for the first time after three weeks, he said he had not forgotten to keep the Sundays between. "Here is my mark," said he, pointing to the roof of his little hut, with seven sticks as rafters; "I count one for each day, and when I come to the last I make the day sacred." Once he asked if he were not very good to remain quiet, and not go out to the war. On being reminded that he only remained at home because he was lame, he answered, "True. I used to be an angry man formerly, and very bold, but now I am obliged to sit still."

In 1836 the translation of the New Testament into the Maori language, a work on which the missionaries had long been engaged, was completed, and was a most important instrument in carrying on their good work, for by this time numbers of the natives had learned to read. Five thousand copies of the Bible were very soon in circulation, the Maories paying for them in potatoes. In 1842 Mr. Williams had the happiness of welcoming Bishop Selwyn, the first Bishop of New Zealand; and by that time the work of the missionaries was so far advanced, that in his first sermon at Paihia, the Bishop said:—"We have come to the uttermost parts of the sea, and even here we find the right hand of the Spirit of God guiding the hearts of men. Christ has blessed the work of His ministers in a wonderful manner. . . . . A few faithful men, by the power of the Spirit of God, have been the instruments of adding another Christian people to the family of God. Another Christian Church has arisen here, in the midst of one of the fiercest and most bloody nations that ever lived, to bear witness to the power of sin over the heart of unregenerate man."

But there were dark times in store for the mission-

aries still,—their influence was shaken to its foundation; only shaken, however; they never quite lost their
hold on the natives whom they loved so well, and for
whom they had sacrificed so much. Through all they
were truly peace-makers, having always the interests of
the Maories at heart, and never hesitating to defend their
rights even when they made themselves unpopular among
their own countrymen by doing so. Those who remain
quietly at home all their lives can scarcely realise what
a hard life, considered merely from a worldly point of
view, that of a missionary is. In the first place he
must leave all his friends and kindred; his native land,
which is never so dear to us as when we are going to
depart from it, never perhaps to see it again ; he must
give up the joys derived from the society of his fellow-
countrymen, and all the countless delights and comforts
which a civilised country offers. In the land of his
mission all will be strange to him. He must be prepared to face danger, to bear hardships, and to devote
himself with unremitting zeal to labours which will
often for years bring forth no fruit. Truly it is a noble
life, and well deserves the support of those who do not
themselves feel called to undertake it. But to those
who are fit for the work it has its reward sooner or later.
Great indeed is their joy when, by the blessing of God,
their labours are crowned with success, and the light of
Christ's gospel shines in a land where darkness had
reigned undisturbed for ages; when the love of the
people they labour to serve rewards them for their
patience and zeal in the good work. The Maories could
not have mourned more sincerely for a chief of their
own than they did for Mr. Williams (then archdeacon)
when he was taken from among them. There is a

Memorial Church erected to him by the Europeans at
Pakaraka, but it is the natives themselves who have
raised a stone cross in the churchyard to his memory.
it has an inscription on it in Maori; translated into English
it is this :—

## A Memorial

### TO

# HENRY WILLIAMS.

#### A TOKEN OF LOVE TO HIM FROM THE

#### MAORI CHURCH.

HE WAS A FATHER INDEED TO ALL THE TRIBES;

A MAN BRAVE TO MAKE PEACE IN THE MAORI WARS

FOR FORTY-FOUR YEARS

HE SOWED THE GLAD TIDINGS IN THIS ISLAND.

*He came to us in the year* 1823.

*He was taken from us in the year* 1867.

# CHAPTER IV.

## COLONISTS IN NEW ZEALAND.

Early Settlers—Colonel Wakefield and
Captain Hobson—New Plymouth—
Maori Discontent—The Election of
a King—The New Zealand War.

IT is not yet fifty years since our first emigrant ships sailed for New Zealand. A company, called the New Zealand Land Company, had been formed, and sent out the settlers, under the guidance of a Colonel Wakefield, to buy the land from the natives—to be paid for in all sorts of things which the Maories valued more: tools, seeds, looking-glasses, articles of clothing, and above all, muskets, gunpowder, and ammunition of all sorts.

From the time that King George IV. unluckily presented some guns to Hongi on his visit to England, the warlike propensities of the Maories gave them a perfect craving for weapons of war so much more destructive than their own. Their native weapons were not very deadly : short javelins and stones flung from slings. At one time the poor missionaries were nearly starved, because the natives refused to sell them any food except in exchange for guns and gunpowder, which the missionaries had resolved not to be the means of introducing in the island. Beads and gewgaws of all kinds, with which Europeans traded so much with the South Sea Islanders, were despised from the first by the New Zealanders ; indeed, their own native ornaments are far handsomer than any imitation jewellery of ours. They value their own green jade-stone—a sort of malachite—very highly, and wear huge ear-rings of it. Polished sharks' teeth they also think a great deal of for adornments. A lady lately returned from New Zealand told me she had been asked two guineas for a single tooth. But to return to the emigrants : all sorts of great people and kind ones interested themselves about them, and did all they could to keep up their spirits on leaving their native land, probably for ever. The poet laureate of that day, Campbell, wrote some very spirited verses for the occasion :—

Steer, helmsman, till you steer your way
  By stars beyond the line.
We go to found a realm, one day
  Like England's self to shine.

Chorus.
Cheer up, cheer up, our course we'll keep
  With dauntless heart and hand ;
And when we've ploughed the stormy deep
  We'll plough a smiling land.

A land where beauties importune
  The Briton to its bowers,
To sow but plenteous seeds, and prune
  Luxuriant fruits and flowers.

There tracts uncheer'd by human words,
　Seclusion's wildest holds,
Shall hear the lowing of our herds
　And tinkling of our folds.

Like rubies set in gold, shall blush
　Our vineyards, girt with corn,
And wine and oil in gladness gush
　From Amalthea's horn.

Britannia's pride is in our hearts,
　Her blood is in our veins;
We'll girdle earth with British arts,
　Like Ariel's magic chains.

Cheer up, cheer up, our cause we'll keep
　With dauntless heart and hand;
And when we've ploughed the stormy deep,
　We'll plough a smiling land.

Before the year was over Colonel Wakefield and his party had bought land enough for a kingdom—as big, it is said, as the whole of Ireland. I wish we could think that the bargains had been made quite fairly, and that the natives had thoroughly understood what they were about when they parted with their inheritance. I fear that at that time, and subsequently, many greedy and unscrupulous traders and speculators took advantage of the simplicity and ignorance of the Maories, and thought only of their own gain, and nothing at all about the welfare of the natives whom the missionaries had taught to trust the Europeans, and that thus much of the missionaries' good work was undone.

The Maories were pleased at first, like children, with the things that were brought them, and satisfied with whatever the settlers proposed, and when they began to understand the value of English money they sold

E

AN EARLY MISSION SERVICE IN NEW ZEALAND.

away their land for that also; but as time went on they began to find out how hastily they had acted. "The money," they said, "which we receive for our land is soon gone, but the land remains with the Europeans for ever." And this discovery was the beginning of endless disputes and difficulties between the Maories and the English, and the poor Maories, as the weakest party, always went to the wall. For a time the missionaries lost much of their influence, and a miserable state of things prevailed.

Then the British Government felt that it was time to interfere, and that it would be well to take New Zealand under its own protection; and so a good and high-minded governor, Captain Hobson, was sent out. He persuaded the chiefs to sign a treaty, ceding the powers and rights of sovereignty to our queen over their respective territories; the queen, on her part, promising to protect them in the possession of their own lands, forests, fisheries, and properties of all sorts. It was very difficult to persuade the chiefs to agree to this, and some of them held out strongly against it. In his dispatches the governor describes how at the great meeting of thirty or forty chiefs which he called together, one of them, named Rerewah, turned to the others, and said:—"Send that man away. Do not sign the paper; if you do you will be reduced to the condition of slaves, and be obliged to break stones for the roads. Your lands will be taken from you, and your dignity as chiefs will be destroyed." Another one, however, called Neni, came forward, and spoke with great eloquence to his companions of the advantages which they would reap by accepting British protection. He then turned to Captain Hobson, and said: "You must be our father.    You must not allow us to become slaves. You must preserve our customs, and never permit our lands to be taken from us." One or two other chiefs spoke in the same strain, and at length the treaty was signed by forty-six of the northern chiefs at Waitangi, in 1840.    And so New Zealand came practically into the possession of the English.

In the same year the Taranaki province, on the western coast of the north island, was founded by the New Zealand Company, chiefly of emigrants from Devonshire and Cornwall.    Here is now the town of New Plymouth, one of the most beautifully situated in the world.    It is built at the foot of Mount Egmont, a mountain with a cone-shaped top, covered with snow, and what are called the sugar-loaf rocks round it.    Near these rocks, some years ago, petroleum was discovered, and a company was formed to make borings for it, but it was not found in sufficient quantities to repay the cost of the work.    Beautiful fine sponges are found on this part of the coast, equal to the best from Turkey, so that, with the hot lakes and springs close at hand, there is no excuse for anyone living in this part of the world not being clean.

It was with reference to this province of Taranaki that discontent began to arise among the natives, soon after the treaty of Waitangi.    The settlers had bought and paid for 60,000 acres of land, but certain Taranaki natives declared that it had never really belonged to the tribes who had parted with it.    This complaint they brought to the English governor, Fitzroy, who had succeeded Governor Hobson.    It was, of course, most difficult for the governor to find out the rights of the matter, but he ended by making the settlers restore a great part of the land. They were half-ruined, and the natives were still dissatisfied.

This was only one out of many such disputes which were continually arising, and the Maories grew more and more discontented with the new comers—or "pakehas," as they called them—and distrustful of the government, which they considered did not keep faithfully to the terms of the treaty. Some unprincipled Europeans misrepresented the motives of the English government, for their own objects, to the Maories, and increased their suspicion. The erections of customhouses and other interferences with their trade were grievances to them, and the slow processes of English law in settling disputes, so unlike their own rough and ready system, tried them greatly.

Things grew worse and worse, and at length a chief, of the name of Heke, with a band of followers, began hostilities in 1844 by cutting down and burning the British flagstaff erected at the Bay of Islands, meaning to destroy with the symbol the reality of the English authority. Soldiers were sent for from Sydney, and the flagstaff was put up again. At the same time, the custom-house near, which had been a great cause of offence, was removed by way of conciliation, but the next year the flagstaff was cut down again. It was rebuilt once more, and this time protected by troops. Again it was cut down by Heke; and this time there was a battle, in which the Maories had the best of it. This was really the beginning of the New Zealand war, for though, after an attack and a sort of victory on our part, peace was proclaimed and maintained for some years, the seeds of the terrible wars of more modern times were sown. The natives learned the art of con-

MOUNT EGMONT.

structing fortifications and fighting from within them which made them such formidable enemies to our troops, although these were always greater in number. The Maories are a brave and gallant people, and the beautiful lands for which they fought were once entirely their own ; and however unwise and unreasonable their conduct might be in accepting the terms of the Europeans, and then repenting of what they had done, our soldiers and sailors, when fighting with them, always felt a sort of respect for them—as men who were, after all, defending their own country.

During the years of peace which succeeded the first little wars, the natives appear never to have been thoroughly satisfied. They felt that the white people were encroaching more and more on their country ; and as the useful things they had brought, with which they had been so pleased at first, became common, and articles of every-day use, they no longer valued them in the same way. The more they learned from the Europeans the stronger they felt, and the more able to govern their own country and make their own laws. Some of them, indeed, stood by the English from first to last—notably the tribes whose hearts had been gained by the missionaries before the settlers came. Some fought valiantly for us, but they were few, and did not represent the true spirit of the country.

The very year when the first war ended the Maories made a land league—a union to prevent the settlers getting more land into their hands. Next they determined to have a king of their own. The English Government did not interfere with this movement, but if it had recognised it and supported it more it might have been better. As it was, the electing of a king was little more than a nominal affair. However, it was done. King Potatau, an old chief of the Waikato tribe, who live among the green valleys on the banks of the beautiful river Waipa, was duly proclaimed, and his successor reigns there still.

The account of the electing of this first king is very curious. In June, 1858, he was formally accepted at a place called Rangiawhia. He entered it preceded by his flag, bearing the device of a cross and three stars, with the name of the country in the centre. After him came the chiefs and numbers of well-dressed natives. He was received by a procession of the inhabitants of the place, one of the chiefs reading an address of welcome. A volley of musketry was fired by an army of young men, who then marched backwards and fell into lines, so as to form an avenue for the king to pass along, saluting him with another volley. The procession then advanced into a square formed by huts and tents, when at a given signal a profound obeisance was simultaneously made by all the assembly of the different tribes to the king. One of the native teachers then stood up and read a part of a chapter in the Bible, and gave out the verses of a hymn, which were sung. He then offered up a prayer. After a few minutes' silence a song of welcome was chanted by one of the chiefs, another volley fired, another obeisance made, and King Potatau was installed as the first king of the Maori race. He did not live long, and was succeeded by his son.

It does not appear that by this king movement any direct hostility towards the English was intended, but the Maories thought it would enable them to protect their rights better. They constantly repeated this sentence :—" The King on his piece, the Queen on her piece, God over both, and love binding them together." Meanwhile, however, fresh disputes were arising at Taranaki about the land there. The poor governor at that time—Governor Browne—must have had a hard time of it between trying to protect the interests of the colonists and of the natives; and as he had never succeeded in learning the Maori language, he often had to trust to the representations of those who did not really care for the native welfare, and it was not strange that he made mistakes. The arrival of the governor who succeeded him—Sir George Grey—gave general satisfaction, but the natives seem to have respected Governor Browne as a straightforward man. They compared him to the *kahu*, or hawk, which hovered over-head, and though a bird of prey still could always be seen; whilst the plans of his successor not being so easy to understand, they said he was like the *kiori*, or rat, which worked underground, so that it could not be told where it went in or where it would come out.

Sir George Grey, however, succeeded in satisfying all parties for a time, but the Maories were really ripe for war, and ready to seize any excuse for it; and in 1863 the terrible campaign of the Waikato—a territory claimed both by the Maories and by the settlers—began.

I met, not long ago, a sailor who told me a great deal about the New Zealand war. He has had a strangely adventurous life, and well deserves the medal he wears for his service in the Maori war. When quite a boy, he went out to New Zealand in the *Orpheus*, a ship which was sent there at the beginning of the war, and which was wrecked on the Manukau bar. He was

saved by jumping from the mast, on which he
happened to be when the vessel struck, into the sea.
He told me of the coolness and courage of the good
Commodore Burnett, and how he had stood waving his
handkerchief while the waves washed over him ; and
how the captain of the forecastle led the ringing cheer
as the ship went down with nearly all on board. No
wonder that those who heard that cheer said that it
sounded in their ears long afterwards.

But the wreck of the *Orpheus* was only the
beginning of the adventures of my sailor friend. He
picked up the native language, chiefly from some
friendly Maories on board one of the ships in which
he served, and spoke it so well that during the war
he was disguised as a Maori, and sent to carry the mail
sixty miles through the enemy's camps. He was then
only seventeen, and must have been a brave boy. They
painted his face a dark colour, and he went safely
through the camp, using the Maori passwords which
he had learned, without being suspected. My friend
remembers with the warmest admiration the bravery of
the Maories. He says he fought because he was ordered
to do so, and it was therefore his duty, but he could not
help a feeling of sympathy with the natives. Sometimes, however, they were guilty of cruel acts, which
of course destroyed this feeling.

I read a description of a native pah in time of war
in a book called "Rambles at the Antipodes." The
author says that a pah, always a curious place, is so
specially when a war drives the natives to take refuge
there. The one he saw covered an area of five or six
acres, over which the huts and store-rooms were clustered
closely, and the whole interior swarmed with dogs,

EXTERIOR OF A PAH OR NATIVE FORT.

pigs, women, and children. It was fenced with a double palisading, eight or ten feet high, strongly lashed with the native flax, and supported at intervals with long posts, consisting of stems of trees, the tops ornamented with grotesque carving. The palisading was amply supplied with loop-holes for musketry. If a pah is strongly fortified, trenches are sunk round the interior of the palisading, in which the besieged can stand in perfect security, and shoot down any one that approaches. The way in which our soldiers got over the difficulty at the battle of Waucka is rather amusing. Captain Cracroft, with his sixty blue-jackets, ran up to it, crying, " Make a back ! " One after the other they vaulted on each other's backs, and again others on theirs, until they were on a level with the top of the fence, and then jumped down into the pah, and before the natives could recover from their astonishment numbers of them were killed.

One incident which occurred during the visit of the author of the " Rambles" to the pah struck him very much. It was in a part of the country where Bishop Selwyn had established daily services in a little church. The natives were busily employed in strengthening the fortifications of their pah. It was evening, and the sun was sinking, when suddenly a bell began to ring. The Maories dropped their tools and left their work, and the whole tribe walked to church. Such a sight must indeed have gladdened a missionary's heart, and repaid him for years of toil.

# CHAPTER V.

## THE NEW ZEALAND WAR.

Heavy Losses—Attack on The Gate Pah — The Maori Chief Tamihana — A Maori Paper—The death of Tamihana.

FOR four years the sad and terrible war raged. The Maories, in spite of smaller numbers and inferior means, held their own in a way that commanded the admiration and wonder of all, and do not to this day consider that the victory was really ours. In fact, however, they were gradually beaten out of the field by the British troops, aided by the friendly natives—" Queen Maories," as they were called—who remained faithful to us. Our own losses were most grievous.

General Cameron, who took the field with a large force in the beginning of the campaign, exposed himself continually, and the natives might have killed him often, but in admiration of his courage, they said, " Don't shoot him ; he's a brave man."

At a roughly fortified pah, called Oraku, containing several hundred natives, including women and children, having surrounded the defenders with an immense force, cut off every chance of escape, and prepared all for a final attack, the general, wishing to spare the lives of his brave enemies, sent this message to them :—"Friends, hear the word of the general : cease your fighting; you will be taken care of, and your lives spared. We have seen your courage; let the fighting stop." The answer given was :—" Friends, this is the reply of the Maori : we shall fight on ake, ake, ake, for ever, for ever, for ever." "If you are determined to die," said the general, "give up your women and children, and we will take care of them." "Who is it," they answered, "that is to die? Wait a little ; our women also fight." "Let your word be repeated," said the general. "Enough," was the answer. "This ake, ake is our last word; we shall fight on for ever." The fight was resumed ; our men made rush after rush at the enemy's works; the Maories were beaten, but, as usual, with a heavy loss on the side of the attacking party.

It is related that when fairly starved out and obliged to retreat, the native chief, Arama, gathered his followers round him, and said, "Let us pray." He then took out his prayer-book, and read some suitable prayers. Then he folded his book in a new shawl which he wore, and said to his men, " Let us make a rush by that place (pointing to a spot guarded by the 40th Regiment), and die fighting at the hands of brave men." His prayers were answered more fully than he expected. A portion of the garrison got safely past the lines of the 40th; the rest, in-cluding himself, were taken prisoners, but were treated with the utmost kindness by our soldiers. Not a single thing was taken from them, not even the new shawl. Good food was given them directly, and a pipe and tobacco presented to Arama, which little attention seems to have touched and pleased him greatly. In this way pah after pah was destroyed, always with heavy losses to the British troops. The account of the attack on the Gate Pah is the most terrible of all. The Gate Pah was a fortification held by about 300 Maories. We had nearly 1,700 men to attack it, and fired into it all day with our deadly Armstrong guns. At length our soldiers fancied the place was taken, and made their way in, when suddenly a party of Maories rushed out of some neighbouring rifle-pits, uttering one of their fearful war-cries, which caused a panic among our men. Twenty-seven were killed, and among them no less than eleven officers, and nearly seventy wounded, of whom many died afterwards.

Of the many heroes, both English and Maori, of the New Zealand war, the one whose history I have real with the greatest interest was the Maori chief Tamihana. His father had been famous for cannibalism and cruelty of every kind, and was never happy except when at war; but Tamihana was among the first to listen to the preaching of the missionaries, and became truly a peace-maker. He was distinguished by a most ardent love for his own people and country, and also loyalty to the queen and the English people. Through his influence the native wars in his part of the country were put an end to, and after he was baptised he made a resolution never to take part in war again.

At the beginning of our war with the natives, he constantly refused to fight with us, though urged in

TAMHANA, THE MAORI KING-MAKER.

every way by his friends and followers; but during the
Waikato campaign he said that if the soldiers should
cross a certain river he should feel that he was absolved
from his promise, and defend his country, as he should
then consider it a defensive war. It was through his
instrumentality that a king was elected; he might have
been king himself, but he had no personal ambition.
He only wished to serve God and his country, and he
chose the man whom he thought most fitted for the post
to be king. He wrote wise and beautiful letters to the
English governor, and if his advice had been attended
to, the war might perhaps have been avoided altogether.
But at that time his goodness and wisdom were not
understood; indeed, as often happens in this world, his
value was never thoroughly known until his death. In a
letter to the Governor of Auckland, he explains why he set
up King Potatau in this way. "The reason why I set up
Potatau as a king for me was, he was a man of
extended influence, and one who was respected by the
tribes of this island. That, O friend, was why I set
him up, to put down my troubles, to hold the land of
the slave, and to judge the offences of the chiefs." He
was most firm in declaring that Waikato belonged to
the Maories, and should be given back to him. "I do
not desire to cast the queen from this island," he
writes, "but from my piece. I am to be the person to
overlook my piece." This idea he never gave up, though
for the sake of the peace he loved so well he made
submission to the commanding officer of Waikato in
these terms:—"We consent that the laws of the queen
be laws for the king, to be a protection for us all for ever
and ever. This is the sign of making peace: my coming
into the presence of my fighting friend, General Carey."

F

After this Tamihana was invited to pay a visit to the
governor, and was treated with great kindness and
respect; but his love for his country was always first
in his mind, and during his stay he presented a petition to the General Assembly for the restoration of
Waikato, but he was not listened to.  He established
a Maori paper, in which there appeared a leading
article in 1863, written by him, referring to this
matter.  "The misunderstandings of two races, a dark
day, a cloudy day, the blue sky invisible, the sun's
rays cannot be seen : the things which make us suspicious, this is the subject we write about.  The
Waikato river does not belong to the queen, but to
the Maori alone.  The things alluded to which make
us suspicious: the sending a steamer up the Waikato
is the first; the bringing up a great gun is the
second; the sending for things calculated to excite
fear; our knowledge that the steamer is made of iron,
and that no notice has been taken of our wish not to
have a steamer sent there.  The word of the governor
likewise to Wi Tako and Heremia, that the flag must
be given up, and the work of the king put an end to.
Although nothing certain was said of the steamer before,
no sooner did the word go forth about one, than a
steamer appeared in the Waikato.  Then first was the
final determination of the chiefs expressed.  'Let
there be no steamer—no road.'  But vain is the effort
of man. . . .  Has Waikato invited the steamer to
come?  We think no encouragement has been given
for its coming.  But let us seek whether there is any
love for your Maori friends in sending it.  Why do
you not bring the cart to fetch and carry what you
want ?  . .  Our lady the queen has given us a

bright word; she said to those chiefs who are not agreeable to give up the sovereignty of their land, of their rivers, of their fisheries to her, it is good; leave the *mana* with them. This is one of our rivers we are unwilling to give. My friends, why do you not confirm this gracious word of our queen, which you have trampled entirely beneath your feet? . . . Truly we believe the word which our ears have heard. You are devising war; therefore you build barracks for the soldiers. Alas! this is your doing, O governor; you do not open the oven that your Maori children may see clearly what it contains. Sufficient that I bring forward the source of sorrow: our friend the governor sending the steamer into the Waikato." It seems sad that such a letter as this should have met with no consideration, but the difficulties were no doubt great.

At the time of Tamihana's visit to Wellington he was already suffering from the disease of the lungs which attacks so many of his race. The troubles of his country preyed on his mind and increased his illness. He returned to his own territory, but only lingered till the end of the year, dying with the Bible in his hands. A most interesting account of this good chief's death was published in a New Zealand newspaper. To the last he expressed a kind and friendly feeling towards the English and the English government. When very near his end, a brother chief asked: "What shall I do, and the Maories, your children, when you are dead?" His answer was: "You must stand by the government and the law; if there be any evil in the land, the law will make it right." During Tamihana's illness none of the usual superstitious ceremonies were allowed to be carried on about him. He constantly read the Bible till

F 2

he became too weak, and then this prayer was offered up
for him by the tribe :—

"Almighty God, we beseech Thee give strength to
Wiremu Tamihana whilst we remove him from this
place. If it please Thee, restore him again to perfect
strength ; if that is not Thy will, take him, we beseech
Thee, to heaven."

So this noble old chief died, carrying out to the
last the principles he had laid down when he set up a
king among his people—" Christianity, Love, and
Law."

The history of the New Zealand war, which must
have wrung the hearts of the missionaries, who had
come among the Maories as messengers of peace, and
sadly diminished the fine native race, as well as
brought desolation to the homes of so many settlers,
and the hearts of so many in England who lost their
loved ones in it, is too sad to dwell on any longer.
It gradually died out, and a long period of peace has
ensued, and prosperity, only marred by the heavy taxa-
tion incurred by its enormous expenses, from the effects
of which New Zealand has been gradually recovering
ever since.

# CHAPTER VI.

## PRESENT CONDITION OF NEW ZEALAND.

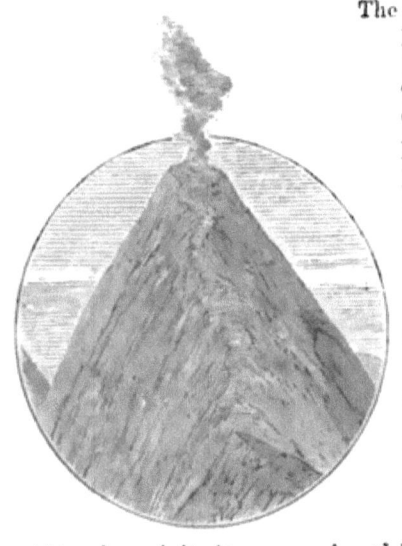

The Geography of New Zealand — Its Forests, Mountains, Lakes, &c. — Lake Taupo—The river Waikato— The Great Hot Lake Ratomahana — Travellers in New Zealand — Its Productions—Otago and its Gold Fields — The deterioration of the Maories—The traffic in Spirits.

IN its present civilised condition, with its beautiful scenery, fertile soil, and temperate climate, there is no pleasanter or more desirable colony in the world than New Zealand. All who visit it agree in this, and those who have been born and brought up there find it hard to be happy in any other country. There are many books, such as Lady Baker's " Station Life," which give one delightful pictures of the free, open-air life of the farmers and their families settled there. Delightful rides through the strange, silent forests, where little is heard but the tinkling note of the bell-bird—rides sometimes for business connected with the sheep and cattle, sometimes only for pleasure,—excursions and pic-nic parties seem to be the greatest enjoyments of life, and being occasionally snowed up, with very little to eat, the least pleasant part of it. These heavy snows, however, are only to be found in the more southerly part of the island.

The forests of New Zealand are chiefly on the mountain ranges. The plains are covered with grass and fern—the splendid ferns about which Bishop Patteson writes with such delight in his letters home. There is a grand range of volcanic mountains, which runs the entire length of the middle island, crosses the straits between the two islands far down under the sea, reappearing midway at the island of Shapiti, and continuing across the northern island as far as the small one called Wakau, or White Island, on the north-east coast. Many of the New Zealand mountains are of volcanic origin, but at present there are only two active ones—Tonganio, in the centre of the north island, and White Island, where the grand precipitous rock called the Sentinel Rock is dedicated to the memory of Captain Cook.

The highest mountain in the northern island is a little more than 10,000 feet, but in the middle island there are higher mountains still. The first peak of Mount Cook is 13,200 feet, and the second 12,300, and there are a large number between 2,000 and 6,000 feet. When we think that our own Snowdon is only 3,556 feet high, it gives us an idea of the grandeur of the New Zealand mountains.

Next to the mountains in size and beauty are the lakes. The largest of all is Lake Taupo, in the centre of the volcanic region in the north island. It is twenty-five miles long and twenty wide, and enormously deep—so deep that its depth has never yet been ascertained. This fine lake has evidently been caused by the subsiding of the ground, as it contains great numbers of trees still standing up in its waters. In its centre rises a small and very beautiful island. Its water is as deep a blue as the ocean, and the native name for it, "Te Moana," means "The Sea." The Maories believe that in the middle of Lake Taupo there

BOULDER BEACH, WHITE ISLAND.

is a whirlpool, inhabited by a "taniwha"—a gigantic kind of lizard, which seizes their canoes, whirls them round and round, and then devours them and their contents. There are quantities of small fish in the lake, which the natives catch, and cook in the convenient natural saucepans formed by the hot springs near. They also use the steam and mud springs for stewing

food.   Visitors to this region always amuse themselves
by cooking bacon, potatoes, &c., in these charming
kitchens.   On the south of Lake Taupo is the pretty
village of Takanu, with a splendid waterfall near—
three cascades, which come tumbling down rocks covered
with woods and ferns.

Some thirty or forty years ago, in this region, a

SENTINEL ROCK, DEDICATED TO THE MEMORY OF CAPTAIN COOK.

whole village was buried; the hot springs had loosened
the hill-side, then came heavy rains, and an avalanche
of mud swept down over the village, and buried it.
I have read many descriptions of the hot springs and
lakes in this part of New Zealand, and most interesting
and wonderful they are.   I think the one given by
Dr. Hochstetter gives one the grandest idea of them.

The river Waikato, which caused so much trouble between the Maories and the English, runs out of Lake Taupo, and passes through a wonderful group of hot springs, extending for more than a mile along its banks. "Then it plunges through a deep valley," says Dr. Hochstetter, "wheeling and foaming round rocky islets. Along its banks white clouds of steam ascend from hot cascades falling into the river, and from basins full of boiling water shut in by white masses of stone; and steaming fountains rise at short intervals, playing two or three at a time, as if experiments were being made with a grand system of waterworks." Dr. Hochstetter counted seventy-six separate clouds of steam visible at once.

The most wonderful part of the lake region is round the great hot lake Ratomahana, which you recognise at once by the clouds of white steam rising from it. Everywhere round the lake there is a seething, hissing, and boiling sound from the numerous escapes of steam, boiling water, or hot mud. Eighty feet above, on the fern-clad slope of a hill, there lies an immense boiling cauldron in a deep hollow with steep sides, full to the brim of perfectly transparent water, looking bright turquoise-blue in its white basin. The surplus water flowing down the hill-side has formed a pure white deposit in a series of stages, each terrace hung with stalactites, and enclosing basins of every size and depth, the upper warmer, and the lower cooler—exquisite and most picturesque baths, the intense red of the bare earth walls contrasting with the blue of the water, the dazzling white of the basins, and the bright green vegetation round. The stone flooring does not cut the bather's feet in the least; it is quite soft to the

HOT SPRINGS OF LAKE RATOMAHANA.

touch, and smooth, so that you can recline in your
bath in the greatest comfort.

Mr. Anthony Trollope, in his book about New Zealand, gives a very amusing account of his visit to the hot springs and baths, which he enjoyed immensely. He was rather disappointed in the fountains and jets of steam, however, which did not quite come up to his expectations, formed from the descriptions he had read; but, of course, they vary at different seasons.

He gives a description of groves of peach-trees in full blossom, and English primroses in flower, at Ratomahana, which seems rather out of character with the great hot lake that gives its name to the place. How happy the pink and blue water-lilies in the Crystal Palace would be if they could spread their great leaves lazily over the delicious surface of the water, and stretch their long stalks underneath! Even the Victoria Regia, the most tropical of the lotus tribe, would flourish there, I should think.

Mr. Trollope tells us that there is perhaps no country in the world more destitute of life than the wilder parts of the northern island of New Zealand. For one long day he rode without seeing a living creature, except one wild cat. That night he slept in a Maori hut, which he had all to himself, and of which he gives a funny account.

"There was a little door, just big enough for ingress, hardly big enough for egress, and a heap of fernleaves, and a looking-glass, and a bottle which looked like perfumery, and the feeling as of many insects. In the morning two old women cooked some potatoes for us, and I rode away, intending never to spend another night among the Maories."

Another traveller, Mr. Crawford, describes his visit to the Maories in this region with his friend Mr. Deighton,

in this way :—" At the time of our visit Takanu presented
a lively scene. The great chief Herekiekie had died about
a year before. His body had been deposited in a small
wooden mausoleum, erected specially for the purpose,
with ´a small glass window, through which the body
might be seen; and the inhabitants of all the surround-
ing districts had collected to celebrate his obsequies, and
to perform the celebrated "tangi," to say nothing of the
feasting. We strolled about the village, and were struck
with the extent of the cultivations ; much was in tobacco, each cultivator appearing to have a small plot to
himself. Here a very ludicrous incident occurred. Te
Herekiekie's widow was squatted crying beside a *picia*
(hot spring.) On Deighton seeing her, he went up as an
old acquaintance to pay his respects. She secured him
by the hand, covered her head with her mantle, and com-
menced a *tangi*. Deighton succumbed, and said to Biggs
and myself, ' You may as well go, for I shall be kept
here for an hour or two.' However, in about half-an-
hour he was able to join us."

In the province of Auckland are the famous kauri
forests,—great pine-trees, which produce a very valuable
kind of gum. It is sold in large quantities every year
for the London market, as it makes an excellent kind of
varnish.

In New Zealand it is only used for making small
ornaments. This gum is not taken from the living
trees, but is dug up from the earth in the kauri forests.
I believe it is not fully known how the gum is formed,
but the Maories say that the sap is continually flowing
down from the healthy live trees under the bark, and
having escaped below the roots into the earth, becomes
hardened into gum. In the great kauri forests it is

supposed that thousands and thousands of tons of gum still lie buried under the earth.

The gum-seekers prod about with long spears, and from the touch know the gum when they strike it. The kauri-trees are splendid fellows, sometimes growing nearly 200 feet high. They do not throw out their branches till some forty or fifty feet from the ground, and the trunks are like columns, not lessening in size till the branches appear. The effect is very peculiar, and must, I should think, remind any one who has visited Cordova of the cathedral there, with its labyrinth of Moorish pillars. The kauris are fast disappearing, as they are being continually cut down for shingles for roofing houses, for which purpose the yellow gummy wood is excellent.

It was as we have seen in the northern island that our missionaries and colonists first settled, but the middle or south island is now the most prosperous, and the most English in climate and in population. Even the scenery is English, except that the mountains are higher and the lakes bigger.

The province of Canterbury occupies the centre of the island, bounded on the north by Nelson and Marlborough, and on the south by Otago. Fully a quarter of the Canterbury province is one enormous plain of three million acres, all divided into sheep-runs, and covered with flocks and herds. Its principal city, Christ-church, is built on the banks of the beautiful river Avon.

The oldest of the provinces is Nelson, with its town of the same name, famous for its hop-fields, and breweries and tanneries, for which the bark of the black beech is used. Otago was enlarged in the year

VIEW OF DUNEDIN IN 1870.

1848 by the New Zealand Company, chiefly by Scotch people, whose industry and perseverance make them generally so successful as squatters and sheep-farmers. The climate is colder than in any other part of New Zealand, but very healthy; and, no doubt, the hills and mountain breezes made the Scotch people feel at home when they arrived there.

It was the discovery of gold fields, however, which made this part of New Zealand so prosperous, and converted the town of Dunedin, then nothing very remarkable, into one of the finest of colonial cities. The New Zealand settlers had long been rather jealous of the Australians, on account of their gold, and large rewards had been offered for the first discovery of gold mines worth working. In 1861 the gold was discovered in Otago, and four years later in Canterbury. The effect of the discovery was almost like the touch of the wand of Cinderella's fairy godmother in this part of New Zealand. Fine buildings sprang up in the towns, gas illumined the streets, railways and telegraph wires crossed the country. The middle island of New Zealand may now truly be described, like her sister Australia, as " the land of wool and gold."

The seat of the British Government is now at Wellington, a large town at the south of the northern island, and at the nearest point to the middle island, so that it, as it were, commands both. From the middle island the Maories have almost entirely disappeared.

It is in the wildest parts of the centre of the north island that the natives are now found in the greatest numbers. The valley of the Waikato, for which they fought so hard, the British have finally taken possession of, but beyond this is a region which the Maori king

still retains as his dominions. In this part of the
island the English can make no roads or put up
telegraph-posts, to the great inconvenience of the

THE ARROW RIVER GOLD-DIGGINGS IN OTAGO.

settlers. Here the Maories make their own laws, and, to
use an expressive but not very scholarly phrase, "keep
themselves to themselves." They seem contented and

quiet, and it is thought will remain so if no attempt is made by the Europeans to encroach further on their rights; and meantime, for the consolation of those who crave to see the whole country under British dominion, there is no doubt that the native race is gradually dwindling away.

It is a melancholy thought, that the various diseases and habits unsuited to the climate introduced by the Europeans, have a good deal to do with the deterioration of the Maori race. The introduction of spirits, for instance, has been most injurious to them, physically and morally. Nothing interfered more with the missionaries' work among them, after the settlers came, than this. A gentleman lately returned from New Zealand told me that he had actually seen a colonist of good position and reputation encouraging and treating the natives to drink, because when they were in a drunken condition he could get them to sell their land more easily and cheaply. It is really difficult to imagine any proceeding, not absolutely criminal, more wicked than this. The natives themselves are well aware of the injurious effects of spirit-drinking.

On one occasion during the war, when about to attack a pah, the friendly natives accompanying the European militia refused to carry some kegs of rum, containing the usual allowance for the soldiers. When the governor urged them to do so, they said they were too heavy. On being reminded that they had offered to carry a four-pounder, and that the weight of the keg was trifling in comparison, the chief said, "The fact was, they did not want the Europeans to have any spirits: that they had need of all their senses in attacking the pah, and if they drank they would lose them."

G

The governor could say no more, and the Europeans went without their grog. And there is another story, almost too sad to dwell upon, which shows the light in which the natives regard the introduction of spirits into their land. Not very long ago, only last Christmas, a terrible murder of a young English lady was committed by a drunken Maori. He was condemned to death, and the governor gave the gentleman whom I have just mentioned a copy of a letter written to him from the gaol, by the Maori, which he has kindly allowed me to print here. This is what it says:—"Go this letter of mine to the Governor.

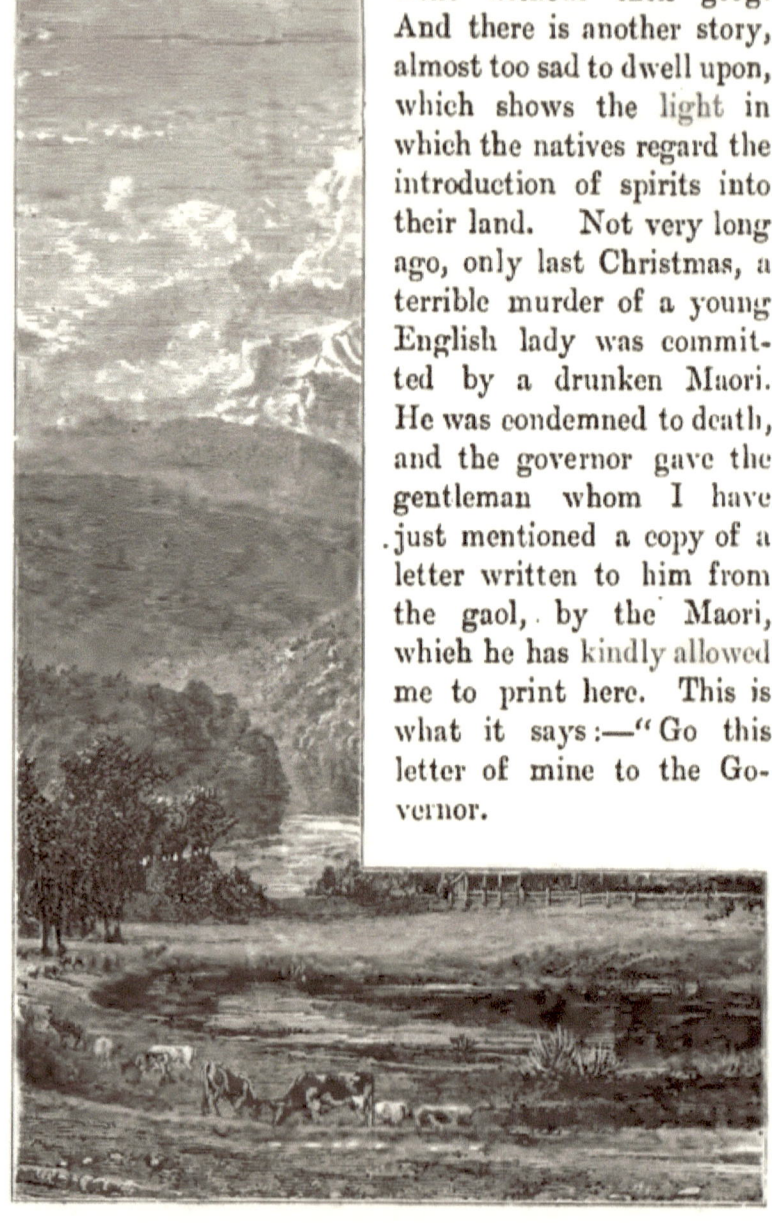

VIEW IN THE VALLEY OF THE WAIKATO RIVER.

" Friend, Greeting.

"I have heard that I am to be put to death on Wednesday, and I am willing to die on that day, but I have a word to say to you. Let my bad companions, *your children*, beer, rum, and other spirits die with me. They led us to commit wrong, and now let us die together, one death on the day that I am to die. It will not be right that they survive that day, but I and my bad companions should die together, lest they should remain to lead people to death, but as I am to die, let spirits die also, do not leave any of its kind in the world, let it be destroyed from the face of the earth lest it should remain to cause trouble to man. Man would then be answerable for his own troubles. If it was destroyed it would be well. Man would then seek his own troubles. Then it would be well, there would be no cause for trouble." That is all, from                          Tuhiata.

I think no Englishman could read such a letter as this, more eloquent in its simplicity than any speech at a temperance meeting, without a pang of national self-reproach. It is so sad that the same nation who first preached to the natives of New Zealand the Gospel of Christ should have let loose among them this demon drink, which has long worked such frightful mischief and misery in England, but was unknown to the Maories till they brought him. On the constitutions of these inhabitants of warm lands strong spirits seem to have specially bad effects; the aborigines of Australia are fast dying out, chiefly, it is said, from excessive drinking. No doubt we have much to answer for as a nation in this matter; but besides all this there seems to be a strange law of nature which we cannot

G 2

altogether understand, which decrees that in whatever land the white man settles the dark native race diminishes, and as it were melts away before him. This law is, as it were, typified in the animal and vegetable worlds. The Maories recognise and acknowledge it themselves—it is a saying among them that—

· " As the white man's rat has extirpated our rat, so the European fly is driving out our fly, the foreign clover is killing our ferns, and so the Maori himself will disappear before the white man."

It is some consolation that the British Government has made more effort to encourage and preserve the native race in New Zealand than in any other of her colonies. A number of them now hold seats in the General Assembly, and have therefore a voice in the government of the country, and not long ago they contributed by their votes to turn out of office, on a motion of want of confidence, a ministry whom they considered hostile to the Maori race. Two of them have been admitted into the cabinet, and assist the ministry by expressing their views on all important questions about native affairs. There are a considerable number of Maori clergymen, and in every British army list are to be found the names of Maori chiefs among the officers of the colonial forces. They are still the largest owners of territory in their country, so we may hope that the day when this fine and interesting race of people will have finally disappeared may still be far distant.

# CHAPTER VII.

## NEW CALEDONIA.

Bishops Selwyn and Patteson—The Bread-fruit — Ways of dressing it — The Natives—Their Houses— Bêche-de-mer Fishing—The Coral Lands—The Chiefs of New Caledonia — The principal native Amusements—The Explorations of Captain Erskine — The first Missionaries—New Caledonia used as a Convict Settlement.

NEW CALEDONIA, a big island lying to the north of New Zealand, is the most southerly of those islands in the Pacific Ocean which are classed together under the name of "Melanesia." All who have read the lives and letters of the good bishops Selwyn and Patteson are familiar with the name of Melanesia.

When Bishop Selwyn was first made bishop of New Zealand, all these islands were included in his diocese, and when Mr. Patteson went out to help him, it was among these that his work chiefly lay. Eventually, they were made into a separate diocese, and Mr. Patteson was made the first missionary Bishop of Melanesia. With New Caledonia, however, he had very little to do, as it is in the possession of the French, who have established their own missions there. When we think about missionaries, we should not forget that numbers are sent out to heathen lands by other branches of the Christian Church · besides our own, of whose work we in England naturally hear less than of our own, but whose lives are equally devoted and self-sacrificing.

New Caledonia is no less than 240 miles long, it is very mountainous, and has rather a bleak, barren appearance. The red clay soil is less fertile than that of most of the South Sea islands, which is, perhaps, the reason that the inhabitants are more industrious than most of their neighbours, and have cultivated the ground more.

The bread-fruit, which is the staff of life to the natives of these islands, is indigenous in New Caledonia, but does not grow in the same profusion as in most of them. The South Sea Islanders have a curious legend with reference to the origin of the bread-fruit. They say, that in the reign of a certain king, when the people ate red earth, a husband and wife had an only son of whom they were exceedingly fond. The boy was weak and delicate : and one day the husband said to the wife : " I compassionate our son ; he is unable to eat the red earth. I will die, and become food for our son." The wife naturally asked how he would become food ; and he explained that he had prayed to his god to help him, and had received a favourable answer. " When I am

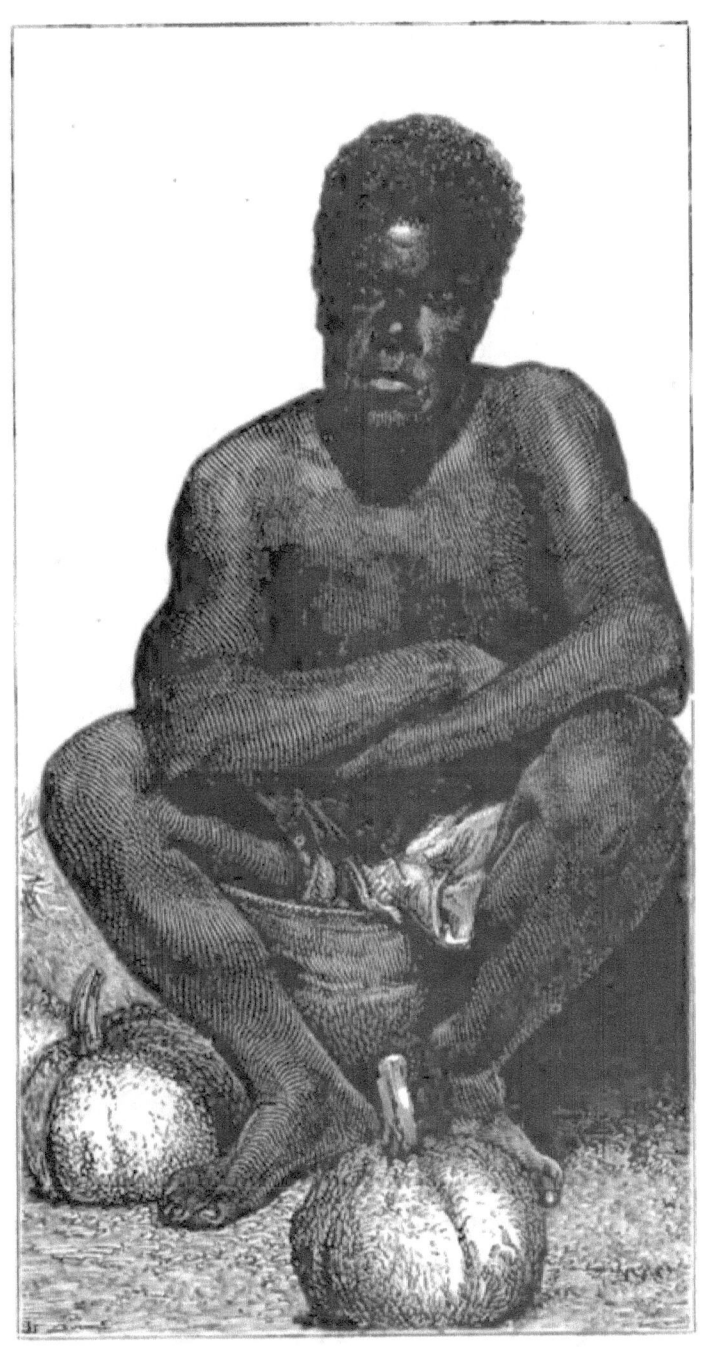

NATIVE OF NEW CALEDONIA, WITH BREAD-FRUIT.

dead," he said, "take my body, separate it, and plant my head in one place, my heart in another, and so on. Then come into the house and wait. When you shall hear at first a sound like that of a leaf, then of a flower, afterwards of an unripe fruit, and at last of a ripe, round fruit falling on to the ground, know that it is I who am become food for our son." He died soon after, and his wife obeyed his directions. After a while she heard a leaf fall, then the large scales of the flower, then a small unripe fruit, afterwards one full-grown and ripe. This was in the night. When daylight came, she woke her son and took him out, and they beheld a large and handsome tree covered with broad, shining leaves, and loaded with bread-fruit.

The bread-fruit tree is certainly a most beautiful and wonderful one. The trunk, which is covered with a light-coloured, rough bark, sometimes measures two or three feet round, and rises from twelve to twenty feet before the branches shoot out. Their form is very graceful, and the leaves are large, broad, and thick, of a dark green colour, with a surface as glossy as the most shiny evergreen. The fruit is sometimes round and sometimes oval; about six inches in diameter, and covered with rough rind, marked into lozenge-shaped divisions, rising in the middle. It is at first a light pea-green colour, then it changes to brown, and when fully ripe becomes a rich yellow. The fruit hangs to the small branches of the trees by a short, thick stalk, either singly or in clusters. The flower is nothing particular. The fruit is never eaten raw, except by the pigs; and the natives have several ways of dressing it. When travelling, they often simply roast it in the flame or ashes of a wood fire, then they peel off the rind and

eat the pulp. Sometimes they plunge it, when cooked
in this way, into the water, and when soaked it becomes
a sweet, spongy paste, of which the natives are very
fond. The usual way of cooking it, however, and the
best, is by baking it in an oven of heated stones. The
rind is taken off and the fruit cut in slices, a layer of
leaves is placed over the hot stones, and the fruit laid
on it, another layer of leaves over the fruit, and hot
stones on the top of them. The whole is then covered
with earth and leaves, several inches in depth. In about
half an hour the fruit is taken out nicely browned on
the outside, the inside looking rather like the crumb of
a white loaf.

Plantains, sugar-canes, and cocoa-nuts also grow in
New Caledonia, but in no great abundance. The
natives cultivate them, as well as yams, with skill and
care. There are plenty of fish on the coast, plenty of
turtles, and a great variety of birds, some peculiar to
the island; but quadrupeds seem almost unknown.
There are no native names for dogs, cats, or goats.

The natives are a tall, well-proportioned race of men.
They have very frizzly hair, which is sometimes tied in
a bunch on the top of the head, sometimes in two
bunches, one on each side of the head, and very often
cut short all round like a frizzly mop. The chiefs wear
a sort of turban-like cap. The men wear scarcely any
clothing, the women have a kind of petticoat.

Captain Cook, who was one of their earliest visitors,
if not quite the first, gave them an excellent character:
he described them as being most courteous and friendly,
and not at all addicted to pilfering. He and his party
were guided and accompanied in their excursions by natives who showed not the least fear of the white men,

GROUP OF KANAKS, SHOWING MODES OF DRESSING THE HAIR.

and never the slightest sign of hostility. Subsequent visitors to the island were not nearly so fortunate in their reception, but perhaps they did not understand so well how to manage the natives. Captain Cook had so much experience in making acquaintance with savages, and such a warm heart and genuine feeling of interest in them and honest wish for their welfare, that he generally succeeded in inspiring them with confidence and gaining their goodwill. His death at last, at the hands of the Sandwich Islanders, was as it were from an accident; though a most sad one. Unprincipled traders, too, constantly removed the friendly feeling Captain Cook had established, and then, though, they might themselves escape, woe to the next party of white men who might visit the spot!

There is a curious story of the wife of one of the French governors of New Caledonia having been left alone in a boat by her husband and friends for a short time, and attacked by a party of natives, who attempted to carry her off. Her weapon of defence was her crinoline—one of the large ones full of steels worn in those days—which it is said saved her from her fate. In what manner she used it does not exactly appear, but apparently in the scrimmage the steel ribs got loose and came to her rescue. Perhaps the natives fairly took fright at the sight of such an extraordinary appendage to a lady's dress; anyway it delayed their operations till the governor and his party came up!

The natives are generally called *kanaks*, but I have read lately that the way in which the Europeans apply this name to them is often incorrect, as strictly speaking the meaning of the word in their language is simply a man; however, it is a more convenient and shorter term for them than the inhabitants of New Caledonia, so no doubt its use will continue. They differ from other Melanesians in having circular houses well and strongly built with a high conical roof. The frame is formed of reeds and spars, covered on all sides with long grass. The entrance is just large enough to permit a man to creep into it, and as it serves also for a chimney, the heat and smoke are intolerable to a stranger, though the inhabitants are little affected by them.

HOUSE IN NEW CALEDONIA.

In this, as in other matters, habit accustoms one to strange things. The native arms are spears, darts, and slings, and a kind of club or tomahawk; the bows and poisoned arrows used in many of the Pacific Islands,

A CHIEF OF NEW CALEDONIA.

with which so many sad missionary stories are connected, are unknown here.

An old friend of my father's had planned an expedition to New Caledonia with a bêche-de-mer fishing party from New Zealand. Some accident prevented his going at the last minute. The whole of the party were massacred by the natives, who had probably received some provocation from the last white men who had visited them.

This bêche-de-mer fishing is the most profitable trade of the Coral Islands, not even excepting the whale fishing. The creature is a huge sea-slug, which the Chinese people consider a great delicacy, and for which they give from £60 to £100 a ton. There are four kinds, the

BUSH SCENE IN NEW CALEDONIA.

grey, the black, the red, and the leopard. The black is the largest, and is sometimes as long as thirty inches, and as thick as a man's leg. Some of these creatures like to lie on the sandy bottoms of the shallow lagoons between the coral reefs, others live on the reefs where the surf is constantly breaking, so that whatever the weather may be, the fishers need never be idle. In calm weather they gather the red kind off the top of the reef just inside the foam of the breakers; in stormy times they dive for the black species inside the lagoon. The bêche-de-mer fishers are generally a wild, rough set of men, but hospitable and generous, and manage to get on very well with the natives of the various islands whom they take with them to do the hardest part of the work. They generally build small craft with the help of the natives, and cruise about from island to island, carrying with them a few axes, some long knives, and two or three great cast-iron boilers for the fish. They often take no provisions but cocoa-nuts, trusting to finding turtle, fish and sea-birds' eggs to live on. A great deal of information about the islands of the Pacific Ocean has been obtained from these men, as they live on them till their cargoes are completed, whereas the whalers only discover their existence.

Mr. Cooper, in his delightful book on "Coral Lands," quotes a verbatim copy of a treaty between English bêche-de-mer fishers and the natives they employ; the natives always liking to have the agreement in writing, though quite unable to read or write themselves. This is how the treaty is worded—" We, men and women of Nukunivano, whose marks are put at the bottom of this paper, agree to go with the Captain Longbeard (their own nickname for the gentleman in question) to the

A KANAK FISHERMAN.

island of Gannet Gay, and to fish for bêche-de-mer, and to fish for six moons, and to be paid each man or woman fourteen fathoms of calico, or twenty-one plugs of tobacco per moon, or other things as we like, such as needles and knives, at the value as we have before agreed; and at the end of six moons to be returned to our homes, if the wind should be fair for us to come back at that

FISHING ON A RAFT.

time. The Chief, whose name is Dogfish, shall superintend the work. The Captain Longbeard shall tell the chief Dogfish what the people are to do, and Dogfish shall tell the people. The Captain Longbeard shall not beat any of the people. The people shall not fight among themselves, but if there be any quarrel among

II

them they shall refer it to the Captain Longbeard and to the Chief Dogfish. If any one of the people die, that which is due to him or her shall be intrusted to the Chief Dogfish, to be given to his or her family. The Captain Longbeard shall supply to all the people for nothing lines and fish-hooks that they may catch themselves food. All food and fresh water shall be taken charge of and fairly divided by the Chief Dogfish. Twenty-eight days shall count for one moon; and of each moon shall be four days' rest—that is to say, the people shall work six days, and on the seventh day they shall do no work. They shall not lie to the Chief Dogfish, or be lazy, sulky, or dissatisfied. There is no more to say."

The people, generally speaking, thoroughly enjoy an expedition of this sort; they all live together like one family, and part good friends. One can well understand a few months spent in this way must make a delightful change in the monotony of their lives. The author of "Coral Lands" describes them as laughing and skylarking as only coral islanders can while they gather the shiny "trepang," as the Chinese call the bêche-de-mer, or spear other fish among the stones. These strange sea-slugs have no eyes, and seem to spend their lives in sucking in water and sand and squirting it out again. When ejected the fluid is poisonous, and if a drop enters the human eye it feels like a red-hot coal, so that the fishermen have to be on their guard in touching and gathering them. The creatures seem to belong to the lowest order of animal life, and yet, blind as they are, if left on the beach separated from one another, they have the sense to collect together again, and the fishermen are sure to find them in one heap when they return. The method of curing them for the Chinese market is to bake or boil them, and then smoke them for about forty-eight hours, when they turn into the firm gelatinous substance the Chinese love, and which if properly managed will keep for a long time.

The New Caledonians are great fishermen, for, owing to the unproductiveness of their land, they have to depend on what they can catch as their principal means of subsistence. There is a kind of small fish something like a sardine, which comes in large shoals, on which the natives live a great deal. In the small rivers they catch eels and cray-fish. Mullet are abundant, and on the beach plenty of shell-fish and molluscs of various kinds are to be found.

The chiefs of New Caledonia are very great people: the natives approach them in a crouching position, and they have the power of life and death absolutely in their hands. They are very superior to the common people.

Their gods are their ancestors, whose relics they preserve very carefully, and they pray to these gods before doing anything of importance—fighting, fishing, planting, or even feasting.

The spirits of those who die are supposed to go into the bush, and at certain periods of the year they have feasts in which they prepare heaps of food for them. They used to think the white men were the spirits of the dead, and brought sickness, and gave this as a reason for killing them. I believe they have quite given up this idea now, but I am afraid it is too true that the Europeans brought them many diseases of which they had never heard before. On the death of a chief there are grand ceremonies of feasting and lamenting, and elaborate tombs are erected for them which are always kept sacred.

The principal amusement here, as in most of the Pacific Islands, is dancing. There is one very peculiar performance called the "pilou pilou," of which I read an account in a French illustrated journal called the "Tour du Monde."

A DOUBLE PIROGUE OF NEW CALEDONIA.

A party of travellers had paid a visit to the island, and were about to leave it, when they were dreadfully alarmed by seeing a long file of kanaks approaching, armed, tattooed and blackened, and brandishing their hatchets, their clubs, and their redoubtable lances: they came nearer and nearer, and at last placed themselves be-

A "FILOU FILOU."

fore the Frenchmen.    At the same time two men seated
themselves on the turf opposite the troops of warriors, one
holding a flute and the other a hollow bamboo, upon which
they began to play.    The travellers at once recognised the
festival sound, and their fears disappeared.    It was a
"pilou pilou," which the chief of the district was offering
in their honour on the occasion of their departure.    The
principal attraction of the performance was a native
ornamented with the New Caledonian mask.    This is a
frightful gigantic head of wood, at the mouth of which the
man who wears it looks out.    Human hair makes a
great wig for it, and its lower part is surrounded by a
net covered with bird's feathers.    The kanak honoured
with the wearing of this advanced towards the spectators
from the sea-shore by way of allusion to their arrival in
the island.    He danced a long time before his comrades,
who accompanied him brandishing their spears above his
head, agitating their arms in time, and making a sort of
panting whistle.    After this exhibition the chief placed
himself in front of the line, and made a sort of address
to the departing guests, with long pauses now and
then, during which the kanaks joined in an ear-piercing
howl.    The address was chiefly a series of good wishes
and kind expressions to the Frenchmen, such as—" Our
friends are going to leave us, they are going to set out
to-morrow on the great sea.    May the winds be favourable to them.    May they find the sea calm and gentle,
and arrive safe in port."

Captain Erskine, in his interesting book about the
cruise of the *Havannah* among the islands of the Western
Pacific, tells us a good deal about New Caledonia, which
he visited in company with Bishop Selwyn.    The Bishop
was in his own little mission vessel, the *Undine*, cruising

among the Loyalty and New Caledonian Islands, in order to collect scholars for his college. The Bishop never allowed any sort of arms to be carried on board the *Undine*. Personally he had no fear at all of the savage races of these parts, whom he always managed to impress favourably, but his crew were not at all sorry to find themselves for once under the protection of an English man-of-war.

On his part, Captain Erskine found the Bishop's knowledge of the languages and habits of the natives most useful in his explorations. They landed at Yengen, on the north side of New Caledonia, where they named the strange detached rocks, looking like ruined castles, at the entrance of the harbour, the "Gates of Yengen." They were most kindly entertained by the Chief "Basset," on whose breast was tattooed his name, at his circular house. It was built on the banks of the river, with low walls about four feet high, and a lofty, well-thatched roof surmounted by a pale, carved and painted red, and ornamented with shells.

It was in 1843 that the first missionaries landed in New Caledonia, ten years before the French flag was hoisted there. A French ship called the *Bucéphale* arrived, and the Captain landed accompanied by five missionaries, who were left unprotected in that great island, filled at that time with a specially cannibal and savage race of people, and where food was scarce and the soil unproductive. The head of the party was Monseigneur Douane, the good and brave Bishop of Amata. The first Christian worship in New Caledonia took place, strangely enough, as in New Zealand, on Christmas Day, and Monseigneur Douane gives a beautiful description of it in one of his letters. In a temple of waving cocoa-nut trees, with the blue sky for its roof, and the singing of the birds in the branches, and the gentle murmur of the waves on the beach supplying the place of the solemn strains of the organ, he proclaimed for the first time the "Gloire à Dieu au plus haut des cieux," while the poor natives listened in profound silence. The troubles of the French missionaries, as was the case with our own in New Zealand, did not begin immediately. At first they were warmly welcomed, the presents they had brought were highly appreciated, and the chiefs were all friendly. Monseigneur Douane soon made an expedition into the interior, trusting himself alone with two natives. He describes with delight the beauty of the scenery,

NATIVES OF THE INTERIOR OF NEW CALEDONIA.

the glorious mountains grand and bare, and the green valleys, and broad rivers often forming cascades. In one place the party had to cross a river broader than the Seine, which, as poor Monsigneur Douane could not swim, was no easy matter. However, he placed himself between two natives, and they swam across with him, supporting him on each side.

The missionaries established themselves at a village called Balade, where the chief had given permission to the sailors of the *Bucéphale* to cut down the trees, and built a hut for them, enclosing a garden, which they stocked with the seeds and vegetables they had brought with them. This answered well enough at first, but when the rainy season came, the wood with which the hut was built became sodden and worm-eaten, and fell to pieces just when the poor missionary needed it most.

NATIVES OF NEW CALEDONIA.

A FARM IN NEW CALEDONIA.

Then came a terrible time of scarcity, and the natives took to robbing them of everything they could lay their hands on. The missionaries were in sore straits, when

CASCADE IN NEW CALEDONIA.

another French ship arrived, bringing supplies, and articles of exchange for them. Among other things the captain left them a huge bull-dog, which the missionaries named "Rhin," after the ship. Rhin was a capital watchman, or rather a watchdog, and guarded his master's property famously. The natives conceived a great respect for and awe of him, and one day the chief of a neighbouring village called, and asked to see him. Rhin was summoned, and the chief made him a magnificent present of yams, sugar-canes, taro, and other good things; at the same time he made a little speech telling him how grand and powerful he considered him, and soliciting his friendship and protection. Later the missionaries procured some more dogs as guards, but Rhin always retained his title of chief. One day a native of a strange tribe had stolen a tool used by the carpenter the missionaries employed. He fled as fast as his legs could carry him, but Rhin was after him in no time, followed by all the other dogs of the mission. The thief vaulted into a tree, and was soon safe at the top; Rhin planted himself at the bottom. Meanwhile a number of natives about, though quite innocent, thought it wise to take to their heels also. As soon as the other dogs saw this they pursued them, barking and biting their heels; the poor natives plunged into the river, and the dogs went after them. Rhin, however, knew better, and never left his post. By-and-bye up came the carpenter, in a state of fury, and proceeded deliberately to cut down the tree in which the thief sat, with his axe. The cries of the wretched man brought a missionary to the rescue, and he was released, making many good promises for the future. Monseigneur Douane and his companions relate many curious stories of the natives. Their very first object of course was to make them abandon their cannibalism. One day a man, half-converted, said to the Bishop, "Father, it may be that eating one's fellow-creature is a bad action, but if you tell me they are not good to eat, you will lie."

Before much progress was made in the conversion of the natives, there were very dark times for the missionaries. They were robbed, and their houses burned down. Twice they were driven out of the island. One of them, Frère Blaise, was killed, and died praying for the men who had killed him. The others barely escaped with their lives, and suffered terrible hardships in escaping. Still these good and brave men would not give up their object, and only waited for more favourable times for returning. They had their reward at last. Before Monseigneur Douane died a large number of the islanders had become Christians, and he had established native Christian teachers among them, who were able to carry on his work. Monseigneur Douane took some epidemic, rife in the island ten years from the time he landed. It proved fatal, but he died at his post most peacefully and happily, with the words "Lord, now lettest Thou Thy servant depart in peace," in Latin, on his lips.

It is marvellous to reflect upon the power of the gospel in taming the ferocity of savages and paving the way for the advance of civilisation. It not only teaches them what is right and just, but wins their hearts to approve it; and thus prepares them to yield a willing obedience to fair and equitable laws. But it is sad to think that often the fair promise of peace and brotherhood, which missionaries have taken such pains to produce, is rudely shattered by the greed of the settlers who follow in their train. Alas! too often, instead of recognising the natives as men and brothers, these traders cruelly drive them from their native woods, and treat them, wherever they meet them, as little better than brutes; thus strengthening, or perhaps implanting, in their breasts an undying hatred of the white man. Happily, in New Caledonia no such deplorable results followed the advent of Europeans. The work of pioneering was now done, the germs of Christian charity had been planted, and settlers were no longer afraid to come. Soon after the good bishop's death, the French formally took possession of the island, which they have retained ever since, and used as a convict settlement. The convicts have been very useful in improving the land, and building public works, as the English ones were in Australia, which country New Caledonia is now said to resemble in many different ways. There are many fine farms now scattered over the island, and splendid coffee plantations. The coffee grown in New Caledonia is said to be specially fine in quality. The stiff clay soil is ploughed by teams of oxen, and the face of the country wears a very different aspect from that which greeted the early settlers.

# CHAPTER VIII.

## THE LOYALTY AND FIJI ISLANDS.

Loyalty Islands, and the Fiji Group—The Natives—Their houses, possessions, etc.—The Fijians and their Customs—The first Missionaries—The Climate of Fiji—Its Natural History—A Letter from a Native.

ABOUT seventy miles from New Caledonia is a group of islands called the Loyalty Islands. They are formed of nothing but coral in an early stage of development, bare and broken ridges upheaved from the sea. Between them are pits filled with sufficient soil to cultivate cocoa-nut trees and yams, but the islands produce but a scanty sustenance for the inhabitants. Their chief product is sandal-wood, which grows in abundance, and which brings the islands many visitors who trade with China in this article. Walking about the coral islands is dreadful work for visitors, their shoes get cut to pieces and their feet exceedingly sore.

Bishop Patteson, who paid several visits to these

A CORAL ISLAND IN THE PACIFIC.

islands, describes one terrible walk of twenty miles; he says that nothing but broken bottles equals jagged coral. The paths are such that you never take three steps in the same direction, and every minute trip against blocks of coral hidden by long leaves and weeds trailing over the path. Often for half a mile you have to jump from one bit of coral to another.

From the two principal islands of this group, Yengouè or Mare, and Lifu, Bishops Selwyn and Patterson brought away a number of boys, who with many others from different Melanesian islands, became scholars at the college founded by Bishop Selwyn at Auckland, and afterwards teachers among their own people. The accounts of many of these boys and young men are most interesting. No wonder that Bishop Patteson became so fond of them. Their devotion and gratitude to him is very touching to read of. They were always willing to stay with him, though many of them suffered terribly from the cold in New Zealand; so much so that at length Bishop Patterson established a college for them in Norfolk Island, where the climate is more like what they are used to.

The Loyalty Islanders are, however, a hardy race, and suffered less than most of their companions. They are the most civilised of any of the Melanesian race, and are now nearly all Christianised. The first missionaries to these islands were Independents sent by the London Mission, who worked among them most zealously, and with most happy results. They had established schools and chapels when Mr. Patteson first went there, and he was very cautious about in any way interfering with their work. Subsequently, by the wish of the London Mission, he helped them by remaining in Lifu for four

I

months, and teaching and preaching in the native language, which by that time he had studied sufficiently for the purpose.

There is a certain resemblance in all the languages of the Pacific Islanders, though there are an immense variety of them, all totally distinct. Bishop Patteson notices particularly one great peculiarity in their grammar. In speaking of something that is going to happen, they use the present or past tenses in a way that is at once graphic and poetical, but I think it must take some time for a foreigner to understand or get used to it. Where an Englishman would say " When I get there it will be night," a Pacific islander says, " I am there, it is night." The one says " Go on, it will soon be dark," the other " Go on, it has become already dark." One of Bishop Patteson's boys would rouse him at five o'clock in the morning with the words " It is night already," meaning, that it was late for the start on some journey. A chief condemns a man to death with the words " You are dead."

The natives of the Loyalty Islands build comfortable houses with conical roofs like those in New Caledonia, and, like them also, they are uncommonly stuffy inside. They seem to have scarcely any possessions. Their principal articles of furniture are calabashes for containing water, which are neatly slung with strings of cocoa-nut fibre, and are really indispensable in a coral island where water is scarce and not very good. They also make rough and strong clubs from the roots of trees, and flat baskets or pouches with the fur of the strange fruit-eating bat, the flying fox. Captain Erskine describes numbers of the natives swimming from Lifu to his ship, the *Havannah*, when anchored near, with these baskets on their heads, shading their eyes and keeping quite dry. Generally they are slung round the waist, like the " sporran " of a Highlander.

NATIVE OF FIJI.

On one occasion Bishop Selwyn and Mr. Patteson paid a visit to Lifu together. They found a number of people waiting to receive them and to conduct them to the village, where the chief and a great many other natives were drawn up in a half-circle waiting for them. The young chief Angadhohua, a bright-looking boy of

NATIVE OF FIJI.

seventeen, bowed and touched his cap, and taking Mr Patteson's hand held it and whispered, "We will always live together." He was dreadfully disappointed that

Mr. Patteson could not remain in Lifu at that time, and, sooner than be separated from him, volunteered to join the mission party. It was an unheard-of thing that a chief should be permitted by his people to leave them; there was a public meeting about it, and a good deal of excitement, but at length consent was given; the spokesman of the party came forward with tears in his eyes, saying " Yes, it is right he should go, but bring him back soon. What shall we do?" Mr. Patteson laid his hand on the young chief's shoulder, answering " God can guard him by sea as on land, and with His blessing we will bring him back safe to you." Five chiefs were selected as a body-guard for Angadhohua, and what good care his kind English friend took of him we can imagine.

The Fiji group—England's latest colony—consists of some hundred and fifty islands of all shapes and sizes, the largest being Viti Levu. The principal town and seat of our government there, however, Levuka, is situated on one of the smaller islands, Ovalau. The Fijians are a Melanesian race, with dark skins and frizzly hair; but brown Polynesians, from Tonga and Samoa, have settled among them to such an extent that their language and customs have been a good deal influenced by these very different people.

The Fijians are, or were till very lately, a most savage and degraded race. It is only quite recently that the practice of cannibalism in all its most horrid forms has been given up by them; indeed, I believe, in some of the islands least known to Europeans it is still practised, but the natives are now, generally speaking, ashamed of ever having allowed it. When, by King Thakombau the present monarch's own wish, the islands were taken under the protection of Queen Victoria, he sent her as a present a club he valued greatly, with which he had in former days killed no less than three hundred persons, whom he had afterwards eaten. This club, which was made of some very dark wood, he sent to Sydney to be decorated before it went to England. It was beautifully ornamented with silver fern-leaves, and was exhibited in a shop window for some time as a work of art.

Another dreadful custom besides the cannibalism is not yet entirely given up by the Fijians: that of burying each other alive, for all sorts of trifling reasons; generally speaking, however, with the consent of the party to be buried. In one of the small islands, where some friends of mine had cotton plantations and lived for some time, an old man insisted on being buried alive, because he said that one of his sons had not saluted him in the morning with the usual reverence, which showed that he was getting too old, and losing respect, and he would rather be buried out of the way.

I have read, too, a well-authenticated account of a young man who chose to be buried alive because he was growing thin, and was afraid the girls would laugh at him. His father and other members of the family assisted in the ceremony quite cheerfully. This story is told by a sailor of the name of John Jackson, who lived among the Fijians for two years, being detained by force. He learned their language, and they were on the whole good-natured to him, though he often had to escape from one tribe to another when he had happened to offend those he was among. Once he very narrowly escaped with his life.

The Fijians have a great variety of gods, most of whom they seem to consider very like themselves in

their tastes and habits. One is supposed to be very
fond of turtles, one of human brains, etc. At Nateva,
where Jackson lived for some time, there was a temple
where the people used to lay various offerings for the use
of their gods, roast pigs and muskets among them. On
one occasion there was a grand roasting of and feasting
on pigs, but Jackson did not consider that he had had
his share. Being very hungry in the night, he came to
the conclusion that it was much better that he should
have a good supper than that the pork should be wasted
on his friends' false gods, so he stole into the temple,
where he knew the pigs lay, and made a meal off a portion of a small one. When he had finished, he remembered that he had not cut the pig in the same way as the
Fijians, and that he would be sure to be found out, so
he threw the remainder of the animal into the bush for
the dogs to eat. The natives were all extremely puzzled
when they found a whole pig had disappeared, but at
length they came to the conclusion that one of their
favourite gods had swallowed the pig whole! An old
priest informed them that Kalau leka (short god) had
condescended to appear to him in the night in a state of
high good-humour, and had informed him of various
favourable events, and thus it was quite evident that his
amiability was caused by his having swallowed the whole
pig, as when he was hungry he was always unpleasant.
The people were all quite satisfied with this story, and
boasted so much of the cleverness of their short god in
swallowing a pig whole that Jackson was sorely tempted
to undeceive them. He refrained, however, for some
time, for fear of evil consequences, but at length, when
he had become more intimate and friendly with the
people, he thought he might venture to tell them the

story, thinking it would shake their faith in their ridicu-

KING THAKOMBAU, OF FIJI.

lous gods. At first they would not believe him, but
when he pointed out the spot where he had thrown the

pig, and its bones were found there, they were furious, and he had to run and swim for his life.

Jackson lived for some time at a place called Somo-somo, in the island of Taveuni. Here the king, Tuithakau, was very kind to him. He called him his manu-manu (bird), and when he made mistakes, or gave offence by his blunders or remarks, always excused him by saying "What could be expected from a white man?" or "a foreigner?" Many of the things belonging to the king were very sacred indeed, especially his pet cock, which no one might touch. Jackson, however, being a white man, was allowed this privilege, and the sacred cock was put in his charge. On one occasion, he went with the king in a canoe, on a tour of inspection to various islands which were tributary to him. The sacred cock went too, but at one place Jackson forgot all about it, and left it behind. When this was dis-covered, all the party upbraided him bitterly with his inattention to his great and good father, as they called the king. A man was sent on shore to fetch it, and had his hands covered with mulberry cloth, to prevent his touching the sacred feathers. Jackson being provoked with all this fuss, remarked, that if the cock were his, he should make it into soup. This observation caused the greatest indignation, and the king said, that if it had been made by a Fijian he should instantly have had him killed, and dined on him, but as it was an ignorant foreigner who had made it, he must be excused.

That voyage with the king must have been indeed a strange one. At one place they threw overboard a quantity of provisions, and were perfectly silent till they had passed over the spot where the god of the sea—nothing more nor less than a large shark—was supposed to live. Wherever they landed they were feasted with heaps of turtles, pigs, and fowls baked, boiled, and roasted, with all sorts of vegetables and fruit.

After supper there was always a grand native dance, to amuse the king and his manu-manu, in front of the house where they were sitting, an immense fire being lighted, so that the performance might be seen distinctly. These native dances are most strange and wild affairs. The dancers form a circle, and utter a loud shout; they then begin to dance, quietly enough at first, but gradually quicken their movements, each man trying to outdo his companions in the strangeness and grotesqueness of his attitudes, twisting his body, arms, and legs about in apparently the wildest manner, but however excited they become the performers always act in concert, and the dance is as regularly carried out as a Highland reel. Sometimes they career round and round the fire, crouching on the ground one moment, and then starting up brandishing a spear or club the next, and shouting a sort of wild song all the time.

Sometimes girls and women perform dances, most gracefully, for they have beautiful figures, and are wonderfully light and agile in their movements. They wear short dresses, made from the bark of trees and dyed all sorts of colours, and shell necklaces, and on their hair, which is always frizzed out into as big a mop as possible, a wreath of flowers. The elaborate way in which the Fijians arrange their hair is supposed to have been the cause of the strange sort of pillow in use among them. This is simply a straight piece of wood, with two little feet to raise it. It is made either of bamboo or hard wood, and is of course miserably uncomfortable to a European at first, but some people get acenstomed to it, though I should think it must always make their necks more or less stiff.

The first missionaries who settled among the Fijians were the Wesleyans. It is frightful to think of the horrors and dreadful superstitions they had to contend with in the beginning, but they were rewarded by the wonderful influence they gained in a comparatively short time.

I have read a beautiful story, of how the wives of two of these good men, Mrs. Lyth and Mrs. Calvert, risked their own lives to save those of some native women, who they knew were about to be sacrificed, according to the awful custom then prevalent, to furnish a feast for the chief of a neighbouring island. These two ladies were alone at the time, their husbands being absent. They heard the awful sound of the "sacred drum" used on such occasions across the water, and determined to try what they could do. They embarked early in the morning in a canoe, each carrying a whale's tooth decorated with ribbons, the usual offering to a chief when a petition was presented. They were accompanied by a native Christian chief, and regardless of the sanctity of the chamber of Tanoa, the chief for whose benefit the frightful massacre was being carried on, they presented themselves there. Tanoa was very indignant, and asked, if they did not know that his chamber was "tapued" to women, but the Christian chief explained their object, and they presented the whale's teeth. Ten women had already been killed, but these brave ladies succeeded in saving three, for after considering for some time, Tanoa announced, "Those who are dead are dead, those who are alive shall live."

On returning to their canoe, Mrs. Lyth and Mrs.

Calvert were followed by numbers of native women blessing them for what they had done, and urging them to persevere in their efforts; and they did persevere, and gradually the dreadful custom was given up.

There is one town called Nakelo, in the island of Rewa, where the people have always abstained from cannibalism. Here there is a missionary settlement. In Mr. Mosely's book, "The Naturalist on the *Challenger*," there is a curious account of his visit to this place on a grand Christian native festival-day, the occasion of the collection of native contributions to the Wesleyan Missionary Society. The little town was full of visitors, every one dressed in his best. The dancing-green, in front of the chief's house, was cleared, and a white flag hoisted in the middle. About eighty young men danced the club dance and the fan dance. They wore fringes hanging round their waists, generally a combination of red and yellow Pandanus leaf (a sort of pine) cut in strips, and black fibrous girdles of fungus. All their bodies were smeared with cocoa-nut oil. After the first dance, a missionary arrived with three native teachers. A table was set out under a tree opposite the chief's house, and they stood behind it to receive the money. Each man and woman marched up in turn, and threw their money on it, with as loud a rattle as possible. Only silver coins were brought, and the people preferred bringing two sixpences instead of a shilling, because they would make more jingle. They were evidently delighted and proud to make their offerings, and about one hundred pounds was collected. After the collection, another party danced; this time the men and boys were painted in all sorts of ways, with three colours, red, white, and blue. Some had one half

A FIJIAN WAR DANCE.

of the face red, and the other half blue; some had the face red, and body black. Some were spotted with red and blue; some had black spectacles round the eyes, and

A TEMPLE OF CANNIBALISM.

so on. They wore turbans, and plumes of red feathers in their hair, which waved and shook as they danced; and round their necks pearl oyster-shells set in whales' teeth. These whales' teeth are equivalent to money among the natives. The white ones answer, as it were, to our shillings, and those which have become red by oiling and handling for a great many years represent sovereigns. While these dances were going on, about four thousand natives were standing round, shouting their war-cries and flourishing their clubs. It was very strange, says Mr. Mosely, to see the little missionary in a battered, tall white hat, holding complete sway over them all.

Except when excited, the Fijians are a very indolent people. A gentleman who lived there for two years says the word he heard oftenest was " Malua," which means " By-and-bye." Among their proverbs is one expressing their dislike of work, which is, I think, very good—

> If you have a great canoe,
> Great will be your labour too.

When the islands of Fiji were ceded to Great Britain, King Thakombau and his two sons, Ratu Joseph and Ratu Timothy, were brought over to Sydney. Thakombau was entertained by Sir Hercules Robinson at Government House, where he behaved with the dignity and reserve which savage people can so often assume when placed in new and strange positions. The only absurdity he committed was eating the soap which was provided for him, mistaking it for some delicate sweet-scented sweetmeat. The young princes were very intelligent. Ratu Timothy was a good chess-player, and often the winner in his games with the ship's officers. On these occasions, he would stretch out his legs, and raise his head with an arrogance very exasperating to his opponent. When the Sydney parliament was opened, Prince Timothy was taken by the governor to grace the ceremony. He wore, on this occasion, a white cotton garment, reaching from the neck to below the knees, and confined round the waist by a fine linen sash, the arms and legs being bare. He looked like a handsome animated bronze.

Only a few years ago, horses and cows were utterly unknown in Fiji. The friends of mine I mentioned before, who were early settlers, had a present made them of some of these useful animals. The sight of a cow filled the natives with awe and astonishment; but nothing could exceed their surprise when they saw the creature milked. They crowded round at a safe distance; and, the ceremony over, many of them insisted on sitting up with the cow all night, believing it impossible that she should survive the operation. The first time **Mr.** and Mrs. H— were seen on horseback, the whole population rushed into the woods for safety; they imagined the man and horse to be one animal of terrific power and speed. Gradually, however, they became accustomed to the sight, and recognising the features of Mr. H—, regained confidence. On one occasion the horse being fastened to a rail, an adventurous native tried to mount him, but not knowing how this was usually affected, he seized hold of the tail, and planting his foot firmly on the fetlock tried to scale him from behind. The horse, of course, resented this treatment by kicking and plunging violently, and the poor fellow was found some time afterwards, stunned and bruised and bleeding, but happily with no bones broken.

The climate of Fiji is pleasant, the sea-breeze sweeping continually over the islands keeps them comparatively cool and fresh even during the summer; but the midges, flies, and mosquitoes, that love the damp, are almost intolerable. Mr. H. made an ingenious contrivance for the protection of his wife. A very wide circular net was hung from the ceiling, which could be reefed up out of the way, but when let down was wide enough to enclose the lady, her piano and music-stool,

A LAND CRAB.

and here she could sit and sing and play, secure from the tormentors.

Insect life certainly flourishes in Fiji; native quadrupeds, except the rat, there are none. There are plenty of frogs, and lizards, and only two kinds of snakes.

J

Fish are plentiful, especially shell-fish, and there is one wonderful beastie, a land-crab peculiar to some of the Melanesian Islands. He is so strong that he can break a cocoa-nut, and in the early morning you can hear him preparing his breakfast with a noise like a series of blows from a pickaxe.

Some years ago, I had the pleasure of making the acquaintance of the late Captain Luce, the commander of the *Esk*, who delighted me with his stories of his various voyages and adventures. Among other wonders, I remember, he declared most positively that he had seen the great sea-serpent himself, so near that if it had been a friend he should have recognised him. He would not send any account of it to the papers, however, because he felt sure he should be laughed at and not believed. In 1866, Captain Luce visited the Fiji Islands, and was very much pleased with the mission-house, and with all he saw of the improvements among the natives, of which a letter sent him by some canoe men whom he had made small presents is an interesting proof. This is a literal translation of part of the letter :—

"We rejoice greatly that you thought of us kindly, and send us things that will be very useful. We rejoiced much on that day that we pulled the missionary to Galoa, to see the man-of-war and its captain, when we got to the side of the ship, we saw the great land guns and admired them, when we looked about we saw the officer standing at the gang-way, and we said, ' Oh ! that one would speak for us, that we might be allowed to look over the vessel.' Then I spoke to him, and he nodded his head, so we then got on board, and we looked over the hold, and saw the men who were in great number and very industrious in their work ; we beheld them and respected them greatly. Then we looked around us and saw the very great guns, and the swords in great number. We saw the chiefs of the ship, and reverenced them greatly. Then we went again on deck and talked among ourselves and said "We young men of this generation were born in blessed times, to see such a ship as this; our fathers saw no such sight, we are living in better times, and we are very thankful for it.

My letter is finished.

We send our love to you, sir, all of us the boatmen.

I am

Thomas Nattembra. Your friend.

# CHAPTER IX.

## THE ISLAND OF TAHITI.

Its Inhabitants—Its Fruits—Europeans living among the Natives — The Native Dress—Their Food—The Climate—Native Manufacturers— The Language — Their King — Christianity in Tahiti.

MY first ideas of the island of Tahiti, or Otaheite, as it used to be called, were taken when I was a child from a certain comic song called "The King of Otaheite's tea-party," in which it is represented as a most frightfully savage place. A lady in the song visiting the King, and accidentally treading on his toe, has her head instantly chopped off by command of the King. So strong was the impression made on me by this rather horrid story, that I have great difficulty even now in thinking of Tahiti as anything but the most savage and murderous of South Sea Islands. The truth is, however, that it was the very first among them which

MATAVAI BAY, TAHITI.

was Christianised, and is now a most peaceful and pleasant place.

It was in the year 1797 that missionaries first entered the Matavai Bay, and were enchanted with the beauty of the island which has been called the Queen of the Pacific. Tahiti is crossed on all sides by splendid mountains, of which the highest is more than 7,000 feet above

ANCIENT TOMB IN MATAVAI BAY.

the sea. In the middle of the island the mountains divide, and from their bosom rises a most peculiar rock. It has the form of a crown, ornamented by a series of points, from which it takes its name of the "Diadem." All these mountains are surrounded by a belt of land, which is inhabited, and skirted by splendid forests. The land near the shore is covered with long grass, a species of convolvulus, and clumps of waving cocoa-nut trees, always a most reviving sight to toilers of the sea as they near the shores of these thirsty Southern lands. In Tahiti cocoa-nuts are so abundant that the inhabitants use them most wastefully. They generally only drink the sweet milk—(a very different beverage— fresh from the trees—to that we find in the cocoa-nuts

AN AVENUE OF BANANAS IN TAHITI.

of London markets,) and throw away the nut with the shell. In the forest grow many other tropical fruits in the utmost perfection, oranges, guavas, and bread-fruit; and, among the mountains, quantities of a large kind of banana, but these are generally only eaten roasted.

The huts of the natives are scattered on the sea-shore, separated, not in villages like those of the New Zealanders.

Captain Wilson,
a great naval ex-
plorer of the day,
who introduced the
missionaries in Ta-
hiti, had paved the-
way for them on
his former visits
to Tahiti, and the
natives welcomed
them with the
utmost cordiality.
The king and queen
Otoo, afterwards
called Pomare and
Tetua, received

(1.)—VIEW ON THE COAST OF TAHITI.   (2.)—MOUNT DIADEM.

them on the beach, and they were conducted to a large oval-shaped native house.

YOUNG MAN OF TAHITI.

The inhabitants of Tahiti were delighted to see Europeans coming to live among them, as, with the exception of one Spaniard, who had escaped from a ship and taken refuge among them, their visitors had hitherto

only stayed
a very
short time.
European
women and
children
they had
never seen,
and when
the wives
and fa-
milies of
the mis-
sionaries
landed,
they were
filled with
amazement
and delight. For
the first few days
afterwards, large
parties kept arriv-
ing in front of
their house, beg-
ging that the wo-
men and children
would come to the
door and show
themselves.

The natives
were not content
with providing the

YOUNG GIRLS OF TAHITI.

missionaries with a house, they presented them with the whole district of Matavai. This presentation was made in the most formal manner by an old high priest, surrounded by all the most influential inhabitants of the island. There is a fine painting now in the possession of one of the families of the missionaries, by a Royal Academician of the name of Smirke, representing this ceremony. In the centre sits a missionary's wife, with a little white baby in her arms and a child in a white frock by her side, another lady stands behind clinging rather anxiously to her husband's arm; the other missionaries, in the coats and gaiters of the day, and the captain of the ship, are grouped round. Opposite crouches the high-priest, with uplifted arm. The king and queen are mounted on the shoulders of two men, the queen with a wreath of flowers on her head; and all round are the dark-skinned natives, tattooed and dressed in their own fashion. At the back of the picture you see the great mountains of Tahiti, and all round the luxuriant tropical vegetation.

The natives of Tahiti are tall and well made, the colour of their skin is not very dark, and their hair, though generally black, is sometimes red or flaxen; it is always frizzed. They have large mouths, flat noses, and very white even teeth. The women keep their skin beautifully soft, by constant use of the cocoa-nut-oil. They wear their hair short. The chiefs are distinguished, like the Chinese mandarins, by very long nails. They are all tattooed like the New Zealanders; indeed, many of their customs are like those of the Maories, and their language is almost identical. The native dress is formed of a kind of cloth, resembling paper, made from the bark of certain trees, particularly of the paper-mulberry.  As this substance is not well suited to resist rain, it is thrown aside in wet weather, and a sort of matting used instead.  The form of the dress is two pieces, one wrapped round the waist, the other with a hole in the middle, for the head to go through, hangs from the shoulders.  Sometimes the dresses are highly ornamented.  Both men and women are fond of wearing flowers in their hair.

In an account of one of the visits of an English ship to Tahiti, I read of the queen coming on board, most elegantly attired.  She wore a light, loose, flowing dress, of white native cloth, tastefully fastened on the left shoulder, and reaching to the ankle.  On her head was a pretty bonnet, made of green and yellow cocoa-nut leaves ; each ear was pierced in several places, in which fragrant flowers from the Cape Jessamine were fastened. The old priest, who was so attentive to the first missionaries, used to wear a glazed hat, and a black coat, fringed round the edges with red feathers.

The food of the common people is almost entirely vegetable.  It consists of the bread-fruit, bananas, yams, apples, and a sort of sour fruit, used to flavour the roasted bread-fruit.  The most general dish is " popoi," made of the coarse mountain plantain, beaten up to a paste with cocoa-nut-milk.  No less than thirteen different kinds of bananas grow in the island.  The only quadrupeds, (as in New Zealand) are dogs, pigs, and rats.  As the dogs are fed entirely on vegetable food, they are said to be very good to eat—something like lamb.

There are plenty of birds, wild ducks, green turtle-doves, large pigeons, small parrots, kingfishers, cuckoos, and herons.  In the forests are many kinds of sweet-

voiced singing birds. There are no snakes, but among the fish with which the sea-coast abounds, a poisonous kind of sea-snake is some-times found, whose bite is said to be mortal.

The climate of the island, which is deliciously warm, and at the same time quite healthy, makes houses almost un-necessary, and the natives build little shelters, in very light and airy fashion. They are merely a

EUROPEAN'S HOUSE IN TAHITI.

sort of shed, like the roof of a barn, supported by three rows of pillars. The thatch is palm-leaves, and the floor is strewn with hay, and covered with mats. Under these the natives generally sleep, but they eat and pass the day in the open air. They go to bed about an hour after dark, and use a kind of oily nut, stuck upon a piece of wood, for a candle. The mats in their houses are woven in a wonderfully clever and dexterous manner, of rushes, grass, and the bark of trees. They also make very nice baskets, and ropes, and lines, from the bark of a tree, and thread from the fibre of the cocoa-nut. Fishing-lines are made from a kind of nettle, nets of a coarse sort of grass, and hooks from mother-of-pearl. Their tools are stone hatchets, a chisel generally made from the bone of a man's arm, and a rasp made of coral, or the skin of a poisonous fish called a " Sting-ray."

All these articles of native manufacture are, however, becoming rare in these days, as they have been entirely superseded by European introductions, for which, on the arrival of the missionaries, the Tahitians showed the greatest eagerness. Indeed, it does not appear that their warm reception of Captain Wilson's party arose from any desire for religious instruction. They very soon began to complain that the missionaries gave them plenty of the *parau* (word), talk and prayer, but very few knives, axes, scissors, or cloth. However, these were soon after amply supplied.

The first great object of the missionaries was to obtain a knowledge of the Tahitian language, a most difficult matter. Luckily, the natives were never tired of helping them to learn words, by pointing to different objects, and repeating their names over and over again, till the Englishmen pronounced them rightly. This part of the business was, however, comparatively easy: the hard part was to learn to string the words into an intelligible sentence. One most successful student of the languages of the South Sea Islands says, that he was ten years in Tahiti without finding out the proper meaning of the word "ahiri," which corresponds with the English word "*if*," but only in connection with the auxiliary verb "to have," as, "if I had seen," etc.

The Tahitian was the first Polynesian language reduced to writing, and the labour of these early missionaries in forming a vocabulary, and inventing a spelling which should convey a just idea of the pronunciation to English ears, formed the foundation on which the more advanced researches into the Polynesian dialects of later times rested.

At the close of the last century, when the missionaries first took up their abode in Tahiti, the natives were in a deplorable condition of ignorance

TAHITIAN CLUB. and superstition. They worshipped idols, they killed their young children remorselessly, and, worse than all, they were in the habit of offering human sacrifices to their gods, especially to their principal deity, Oro, who was nothing but a straight log of hard wood, six feet long, and decorated with feathers. Most of their idols were simply shapeless pieces of wood, from one to four feet long, covered with finely-braided cocoa-nut fibre, and ornamented with scarlet feathers.

NATIVE HOUSE IN TAHITI.

The missionaries had to endure great hardships and persecutions after the novelty of their arrival had worn off, and some of them left the island in fear of their lives; but when those who remained had learned enough of the language to be able to preach in it, and translate the Bible, and establish schools, their progress was most wonderful:—in a very few years the people began to listen and believe. Fifteen years after they landed, to their great joy, King Pomare himself declared his belief in the true God, and was baptised. He had for some time past begun to show contempt for the idols and superstitions of his ancestors, and his subjects had watched the change in his mind with the deepest interest and apprehension.

On one occasion a turtle was brought him for a present. Now turtles had always been considered specially sacred animals, and were dressed with sacred fire within the precincts of the temple, part of them being always offered to the idol. The attendants were about to carry this turtle to the temple, when, to their amazement, the king called them back, and told them to prepare an oven, to bake it in his own kitchen and serve it up! He could hardly persuade the people that he was in earnest, and when at last he succeeded, they were filled with terror and consternation; and when the king sat down to eat the turtle, they stood by expecting to see him fall down dead when he tasted the first morsel. No one else could be induced to partake of it, and it was long before the people could believe that no special misfortune would follow the sacrilege! For a long time afterwards any troubles that came to the king, who was at one time an exile from Tahiti, were attributed to his Christian inclinations. Not long after Pomare had declared his faith, a powerful priest called Potii publicly burned the idols he had worshipped, throwing them one by one into the flames, calling out its name and pedigree, and expressing the greatest regret at ever having believed in it; and from this time the progress of divine truth among the natives was so rapid, that in the year

K

1814 five or six hundred had renounced idol-worship,
and the following year it was totally overthrown.

A missionary clergyman of the name of Ellis gives a
delightful account of his arrival in Tahiti with his wife
and baby two years later; and of the state of things he
found there.   He describes the enchanting beauty of the
island as he entered the Matavai Bay, with its broken,
stupendous mountains, and rocky precipices, clothed with
every variety of verdure, from the moss of the jutting
promontories on the shore, to the deep and rich foliage
of the bread-fruit tree, the oriental luxuriance of the
tropical pandanus, or the waving plumes of the lofty and
graceful cocoa-nut grove.   "The scene was enlivened,"
he writes, " by the waterfall on the mountain's side, the
cataract that chafed along its rocky bed in the recesses
of the ravine, or the stream that slowly wound its way
through the cultivated and fertile valleys."

The natives soon came on board to welcome Mr.
Ellis, including the king, who was delighted with some
cattle which he had brought from Australia, and
especially with a horse which was given him ; the first
that had ever been seen in Tahiti, and whose appearance
caused the utmost excitement.   The poor animal, which
had been hung in slings and unable to lie down during
the chief part of the voyage, was hoisted out of the hold
to be taken on shore in a large pair of canoes, which the
king had ordered for the purpose.   While the horse was
suspended during the transition, some of the bandages
gave way, and he slipped through the slings and fell
into the sea !  He instantly rose to the surface, and
swam, snorting, towards the shore.   As soon as the
natives saw this, they plunged into the water and
followed him like a shoal of porpoises, seizing his mane

and tail, and nearly drowning the poor animal in spite of the king's shouts to them to leave him alone. However, he managed to gain the beach, and as he rose out of the water, the natives on the shore fled in the utmost fright, climbing the trees, and crouching behind the rocks and bushes for safety. The next morning, crowds assembled to see the captain of the ship mount the horse, with which sight the natives were delighted. They called the horse "a man-carrying pig."

Mr. Ellis describes his first Sunday at Tahiti with great interest and pleasure. Between 400 and 500 natives assembled for the service held by the missionaries in their roughly-built school-house, at sunrise. They were all neat and clean, the heads of the men uncovered, their hair cut and combed, and their beards shaven; they wore the graceful native dress, with their arms bare. Most of the women wore elegant little bonnets made of bright yellow cocoa-nut leaves, but some of them had only flowers in their hair, generally the sweet-scented Cape-jessamine. Some of the chief women wore two or three fine native pearls, fastened together with finely-plaited human hair, hanging from one ear, and a flower from the other. They all sang hymns in the native language, and listened most attentively to the sermon.

In the following week Mr. Ellis accompanied one of the missionaries to the opposite side of the island, and was entertained in the house of a chief, with a meal in the native fashion. The party sat down on the dry grass which covered the floor, and a broad leaf of the hibiscus was handed to each for a plate, with the downy side underneath. By these plates a small cocoa-nut shell of salt water was placed for each person. Quan-

K 2

A VIEW IN TAHITI.

tities of fine large bread-fruit, roasted on hot stones, were now peeled and brought in, and a number of fish, that had been wrapped in plantain leaves and broiled in the embers, were placed by them. Grace was said, and then a bread-fruit and a fish was handed to each individual. The natives dipped every mouthful of bread-fruit or fish into the salt water, without which flavour they would have thought it very unsavory.

The spread of Christianity in Tahiti is one of the most interesting and wonderful of missionary records. In the space of less than twenty years from the time of the landing of the Europeans, it became a Christian instead of a heathen country. The dreadful custom of destroying the chief number of the babies born was entirely given up, and the idols nearly all burned. It is a curious thought, that the greater part of the children growing up round them, whom the missionaries taught, really owed their very existence to their influence. Once at a large meeting of missionaries and Christian natives, an old chief rose, and addressed the assembly with much gesticulation and excitement. Comparing the past with the present state of the people, he said :—

"I was a mighty chief; the spot on which we are now assembled was by me made sacred for myself and family. Large was my family, but I alone remain ; all have died in the service of Satan, they knew not this good word which I am spared to see. My heart is longing for them, and often says within me, Oh ! that they had not died so soon. Great are my crimes. I am the father of nineteen children, *all of them I have murdered*, now my heart longs for them. Had they been spared they would now have been men and women, learning and knowing the word of the true God."

This speech well exemplifies the true Christian spirit with which its author was imbued. He is not content that himself alone should be saved, but his heart is enlarged, and goes forth in unselfish longing that all he knows may share with him the deep inward joy that follows the reception of the gospel of peace. What a contrast between his present moral state, and the black ignorance and crime that formerly reigned in his heart! How such experiences as this should spur us on to spread, to the ends of the world, the glad tidings of the gospel, to the end that everywhere "the people that live in darkness" may "see a great light."

# CHAPTER X.

## THE SANDWICH ISLANDS.

Position—Beauty of Kilauea, the Volcano — Earthquakes — Captain Cook — Death of — King Kamehameha—Introduction of Christianity—Food — Lahaina— Father Damiens.

THE Sandwich Islands are the only important group in the North Pacific Ocean. They are completely isolated, being 2,350 miles from San Francisco, the nearest part of the American coast, and about the same distance from the coast of Japan, from the Marquesas and the Samo Islands to the south, and to the Aleutian Islands a little west of north. They are only connected with the other Pacific islands by bare coral reefs, the nearest of which is about seven hundred miles off. This very central position in mid-ocean, where they are, as it were, a stepping-stone between two worlds, gives the Sandwich Islands much political and commercial importance, and

as a place of rest and refreshment for the large fleet
of whalers in the Northern Pacific, they are of great
value. But besides their advantages of situation, these
Sandwich Islands are in themselves most attractive. All

KING KALAKAUA.

travellers agree in their descriptions of their delights.
All the beauties and enjoyments of the summer island-
world seem concentrated in them, without its frequent
drawbacks, for the Sandwich Islands have long been
civilised and Christianised, and the present king, Kalakaua, who lately paid a visit to England, is a courteous,
educated gentleman, whose great aim is to introduce
modern manners and customs among his people, and
give them the advantages of education and of good
government. The group consists of seven large islands,

all inhabited, and four rocky islets. Hawaii, the largest
of the group, is seventy miles across, being in size and
shape very like the county of Devonshire, but its
enormous volcanic mountains, some nearly 14,000 feet
high, give it a very different aspect. Hilo, the principal town in Hawaii, is one of the most delightful
places in the world. The crescent-shaped bay, said
to be the most beautiful in the Pacific, is fringed
with cocoa-nut and palm trees, and the town beyond
looks from the sea like one mass of greenery, for the
white houses are half-buried in the rich, luxuriant vegetation. It is said, that if a shower falls anywhere
in the Pacific Ocean it may be traced to Hilo; and
these continual rainfalls keep the grass, and the trees,
and the creepers dazzlingly green, and fill the streams
which come leaping down the rocks in endless cascades,
while the rich soil, and the heat, and the sunshine com-
bine to make the whole place a garden. Over all tower
the two great volcanic mountains, Mauna Kea and
Mauna Loa, crowned with almost perpetual snow, which
Miss Bird, in her delightful book about the Sandwich
Islands, describes in this way:—"Mauna Kea from
Hilo has a shapely aspect, for its top is broken into
peaks, said to be the craters of extinct volcanoes; but
my eyes seek the dome-like curve of Mauna Loa with
far deeper interest, for it is as yet an unfinished mountain. It has a huge crater on its summit 800 feet
in depth, and a pit of unresting fire on its side; it
throbs, rumbles, and palpitates; it has sent forth floods
of fire over all this part of Hawaii, and at any moment
it may be crowned with a lovely light, showing that its
tremendous forces are again in activity."

The great volcano of Kilauea, on the eastern ascent

of Mauna Loa, is the largest active volcano in the world. The crater does not send up any smoke, only a thin sort of vapour rises from it, and hangs above it like a silvery cloud; so that, except on the occasion of a great eruption, nothing can be seen of it in the distance. Many adventurous travellers, however, have made the ascent of Mauna Loa, which is one of immense fatigue and difficulty, and have looked down into the wonderful, awful crater. Many vivid descriptions have been written of this fiery abyss, none more thrilling than that of Miss Bird, but all agree that no words can give any adequate idea of this burning, seething gulf of liquid fire, some nine miles round, and perhaps 1,000 feet deep. The brink being reached, the opposite side cannot be seen, so that the awful chasm seems illimitable, and the clouds of red vapour continually rising, and the fire-fountains playing round about, are reflected in the sky, and make the heavens themselves seem on fire. In olden times the Hawaiians believed that in this terrible abode dwelt their great goddess " Pélé," who sported with her attendant demons among the sulphurous waves. There is a curious deposit found in the crevices of the vast lava-hill below the crater, which is still called " Pélé's hair." It is of a yellowish-brown colour, like coarse spun glass. During an eruption, when the fire-fountains play to a great height, and the lava is thrown about in all directions, the wind catches it and blows it out in long thin threads, which stick to projecting points, and thus this curious-looking substance is formed.

There have been many terrible earthquakes in Hawaii, some of which are remembered by the present inhabitants. Miss Bird gives us a very interesting

VOLCANO OF MAUNA LOA.

account of some of these, as told her by eye-witnesses. In 1868 a series of earthquakes began in the month of March, becoming more frequent and startling from day to day, till, as one lady expressed it to her, "the island quivered like the lid of a boiling pot nearly all the time between the heavier shocks. The trembling was like that of a ship struck by a heavy wave." This state of things lasted for a week, and then came the climax on a lovely April day. "The crust of the earth rose and sank like the sea in a storm ; rocks were rent, mountains fell, buildings and their contents were shattered, trees swayed like reeds, animals were scared, and ran about demented ; men thought that the Judgment had come. The earth opened in thousands of places, the roads in Hilo cracked open, horses and their riders and people afoot were thrown violently to the ground; it seemed as if the rocky ribs of the mountains and the granite walls and pillars of the earth were breaking up. At Kilauea the shocks were as frequent as the ticking of a watch. In Kau, south of Hilo, they counted 300 shocks on that direful day. . . . . An avalanche of red earth burst from the mountain-side, throwing rocks high into the air, swallowing up houses, trees, men, and animals; and travelling three miles in as many minutes, burying a hamlet, with thirty-one inhabitants and 500 head of cattle. The people of the valleys fled to the mountains, which themselves were splitting in all directions ; and collecting on an elevated spot, with the earth reeling under them, they spent the night of April 2nd in prayer and singing. Looking towards the shore, they saw it sink, and at the same moment a wave, whose height was estimated at from forty to sixty feet, hurled itself upon the coast, and receded five times, destroying whole villages, and even strong stone houses, with a touch, engulfing for ever forty-six people who had lingered too near the shore." After this awful day, the earthquakes still continued, and people putting their ears to the ground fancied they could hear the imprisoned lava sea rushing below. At length, after travelling under ground for twenty miles, it burst forth with tremendous force and fury. Four huge fountains boiled up, throwing crimson lava, and rocks weighing many tons, to a height of from 500 to 1,000 feet. A gentleman, who was near the spot at the time, described the scene to Miss Bird in these words:—"From these great fountains to the sea flowed a rapid stream of red lava, rolling, rushing, and tumbling, like a swollen river, bearing along in its current large rocks, that made the lava foam as it dashed down the precipice, and through the valley into the sea, surging and roaring throughout its length like a cataract, with a power and force perfectly indescribable. It was nothing less than a *river of fire*, from 200 to 800 feet wide, and twenty deep, with a speed *varying from ten to twenty-five miles an hour*." These descriptions are terrible enough. Considering the awful nature of the volcanic eruptions and earthquakes in Hawaii, however, the destruction of human life does not seem to have been so great as one would have feared would have been the case.

It was at Hawaii that our great navigator, Captain Cook, met with his death—a circumstance as much deplored by the Sandwich Islanders of the present day as by his own countrymen. To Captain Cook is accorded the honour of having discovered these islands, but there are native traditions of much earlier white visitors, and there is no doubt that Spanish navigators landed there in the sixteenth century. However, our first authentic information about them was brought by Captain Cook, who, with his two ships, the *Resolution* and *Discovery*, approached the two most westerly of the islands— Kauai and Niihau—in January, 1778. Great was the amazement of the first natives who went to examine the ships at what they saw. In those days English seamen used to wear cocked hats; these the Sandwich Islanders thought were a part of their heads, and they described the visitors as having "heads horned like the moon." They stated, moreover, that they had fires burning at their mouths—no doubt meaning cigars—and that they took anything they wanted out of their bodies: such was the idea conveyed by the civilised institution of pockets. All these circumstances, combined with the strange language of the new-comers and the firing of some guns, made the natives come to the conclusion that their visitors were certainly gods. There was a belief in the islands at that time that a certain much-honoured god called " Lono " had sailed away in a fit of jealousy and a triangular canoe, having first prophesied that he would return in after-times " on an island bearing cocoa-nut trees, swine, and dogs." Captain Cook's ships, so much larger than their own canoes, and with tall masts, now appeared to the natives like floating islands with trees on them, and they made sure that " Lono " was returning to his own country. When Captain Cook landed, they came to the conclusion that he must be the great god himself. They prostrated themselves before him, and brought everything they could collect in the way of food as offerings. Captain Cook does not seem to have discouraged the idea that he was a god. He felt that it insured the safety of himself and his crew, and for a fortnight the ships remained at the islands, all living in clover. Then they sailed away. Early the following year they returned, and Captain Cook landed, confident of another welcome, on the western side of Hawaii. Here, his fame having spread from island to island, he was again received with divine honours, all the offerings the natives were accustomed to make to their gods being brought to him. The king visited him, and threw over him his own cloak, and presented him with pigs and fruit, concluding the interview by changing names with him—a ceremony which was considered the greatest possible sign of friendship and respect. For a time all went well, as before, but gradually doubts of the divine origin of the visitors began to rise in the native mind. One of them died and was buried; this showed him to be only mortal, like themselves. They began to grudge the supplies for the ships which they had to produce. A quarrel arose between the natives and the seamen, and some of the latter were pelted with stones. Soon after this the ships set sail; they were becalmed within sight of land for a day, and the king sent on board a parting present of pigs and vegetables. All might now have been well, but unhappily the ships encountered a heavy gale, and put back a week later into the Bay of Kealakeakua for repairs, and this time the welcome received by the Englishmen was not nearly as warm as before. Soon some thefts were committed by natives visiting the ships, who could no longer resist stealing pieces of iron, for which the Pacific islanders in those days craved far more than for gold. Then some shots were fired from the *Discovery* at a canoe. This

MONUMENT TO CAPTAIN COOK.

quarrel was nominally made up, but soon after one of the *Discovery's* cutters moored to a buoy was stolen by a chief. Captain Cook was determined that this boat should be restored, and, trusting to the veneration in which he was held, he went on shore, with the intention of bringing the king back with him, and keeping him as a hostage till the stolen property, so valuable to him, should be given back. The king, it appears, would have consented to this plan, and walked to the shore with Captain Cook; but the islanders would not submit to what they considered not only a great indignity but a great risk. They surrounded the king, and protested against his going on board the ships. His wife, too, entreated him to stay. While the king hesitated, there came a cry that the foreigners had fired at a canoe and killed a chief. Then the natives began to arm themselves with clubs, stones, and spears. The king sat down, and Captain Cook walked towards his boat. As he walked, a native attacked him with a spear, and Captain Cook turned and shot him with his double-barrelled gun. Stones were then thrown, and the sailors in the boats, seeing this, fired on the people. Captain Cook tried to stop this, but the noise was so great that he could not make himself understood; and meanwhile a chief approached from behind and stabbed him in the back. Captain Cook fell into the water, and never spoke again. This is the English account of the death of the great navigator, as handed down from Captain King, his companion. The native account differs little from it, except in stating that the warrior-chief who attacked Captain Cook had no intention of killing him, still believing him to be the god "Lono" and immortal, but that, being struck, he gave

L

a cry or groan, which dispelled the belief in his divinity, and the chief therefore killed him. The remains of Captain Cook were subsequently restored to his friends, and he was buried at sea—with what sad and awe-stricken feelings one can well imagine—and the exploring ships sailed away from the bay without the guiding spirit which had brought them there. The work of the great navigator was done, and he lay at rest in the bosom of the mighty ocean whose mysteries he had so long loved to unravel, leaving behind him a name which has since become a household word in every English home.

For nearly a hundred years after Captain Cook's death the spot where he fell was only marked by a cocoa-nut stump set up on a bed of stones and broken lava, on which different visitors fixed sheets of copper with simple inscriptions recording the event. Within the last few years, however, a more suitable monument has been erected by some of his fellow-countrymen.

For some time after the tragedy in Kealakeakua Bay the Sandwich Islands were naturally avoided by white people, but gradually English and American trading ships ventured to approach them again. They were on the whole made welcome, and friendly relations were once more established with the islanders. At length, thirteen years after Captain Cook's death, two English surveying ships, the *Discovery* and the *Chatham*, once more entered the fatal bay. They were commanded by Captain Vancouver, who had been one of Captain Cook's party when he first discovered the Sandwich Islands, and who was a good as well as a great man. The natives must have been alarmed at the familiar

appearance of the *Discovery* once more approaching their
shore, but Captain Vancouver came in no spirit of vengeance. Instead of bringing the retributive fire of guns
they feared, he entered the bay with every overture of
peace, afterwards coasting along the different islands, and
distributing garden-seeds and carpenters' tools, and all sort
of simple but most useful gifts. He gained great respect
and influence with the islanders, and everywhere tried to
make peace among them. At that time civil wars were
rife in the islands. He was not very successful in
subduing these, but he had the great pleasure of making
up a quarrel between the King of Hawaii, Kaméhaméha,
and his young wife, and joining their hands on the deck
of the *Discovery* after a long separation. The history of
this king is a very remarkable one. At the time of
Captain Cook's first visits to the Sandwich Islands each
island had its separate king and chiefs, as had been the
case, according to the bardic traditions, for some 500
years. The consequence of this arrangement was, of
course, endless dissensions and wars. Kaméhaméha,
being a man of wonderful energy and strength of
character, as well as very ambitious, determined to bring
all the islands into his own jurisdiction, and succeeded
in conquering them all, and establishing a thoroughly
national feeling among them ; after which, he devoted
himself to the advancement of his kingdom, and during
his long reign of twenty-five years it may be said to
have passed from a savage to a civilised condition. He
begged his friend Vancouver to get teachers of Christianity sent out from England, and his wishes were
duly conveyed there, but were not attended to. It
is supposed that this neglect was occasioned by the pre-
occupation of England at that time with the terrors

L 2

of the French Revolution, then going on. Kaméhaméha never became a Christian, nor did he nominally give up worshipping his idols, but he abolished many savage and heathenish customs, and paved the way for the wonders worked during the reign of his son Liholiho. Liholiho was in character utterly unlike his father, indolent and pleasure-loving; and though he quite saw the folly of making hideous wooden gods and worshipping them, and the inconvenience of the "tabu," which rendered all kind of useful things useless, was too weak to put an end to these absurdities himself, especially as there was great risk in losing his throne, if not his life, by doing so. The queen-dowager, his step-mother, however, threw her powerful influence into the scale, and strengthened his hands in every way, being well supported by other great ladies, and he lived to see all the idols cast away and destroyed. This was done six months before the landing of some American missionaries, who were the first to carry the Gospel tidings to the Sandwich Islands. They were warmly welcomed by the natives, especially by the dowager queens, of whom there were at that time two, and by a former high-priest, Hewahewa, who with high-minded conscientiousness had thrown up the office he believed to be a false one, though it deprived him of a great position, next, in fact, to that of the reigning king. "I knew," he said, "that the wooden images of our deities, carved by our own hands, were incapable of supplying our wants ; but I worshipped them because it was the custom of our fathers. My thoughts have always been that there is one only great God dwelling in the heavens." There are many most interesting stories connected with the Christianising of the Sandwich Isles.

One brave woman, called Kapiolani, the wife of a chief, who had become a Christian, by way of proving her contempt for the imaginary goddess " Pélé," who lived in the burning mountain, determined to make a pilgrimage there and brave her wrath. She took a journey of a hundred miles over the rugged lava, with a large body of followers. A priestess of " Pélé " met her, and threatened her with the awful vengeance of the goddess, but she was not to be frightened. Near the crater of Kilauea grew a great quantity of a kind of berry, called "ohelos." These used to be considered sacred to the goddess " Pélé," and it was the custom for people visiting the volcano, before eating the berries themselves, to throw some down the crater, saying, " Pélé, here are your ohelos." Without going through this ceremony, it would have been thought impossible to eat them without incurring some dreadful catastrophe. Kapiolani, however, in spite of the priestess's warnings, proceeded to eat them without offering any to Pélé, to the amazement of her companions. She then approached the crater, and, standing there on the wild, burning mountain, and looking down into the gulf of fire, spoke words like these to the people round her :—

" Jehovah is my God; He kindled these fires. I fear not Pélé. If I perish by the anger of Pélé, then you may fear the power of Pélé; but if I trust in Jehovah, and he should save me from the wrath of Pélé when I break through her tabus, then you must fear and serve the Lord Jehovah. All the gods of Hawaii are vain. Great is Jehovah's goodness in sending teachers to turn us from these vanities to the living God and the way of righteousness. . . ."

How the missionaries must have rejoiced when they heard of this brave and noble deed!

In 1824, King Kaméhaméha and his young wife, Tamehamalu, visited England, where they met with every possible attention and kindness. The English government appointed a gentleman to look after them and provide for their comfort, and they were entertained by many of the great people of the day, and created great interest. An aunt of mine remembers seeing them at a garden-party—or, as it used to be called in those days, a "breakfast"—at Fulham. It was at Hurlingham, now famous for pigeon and polo matches, in those days the residence of Mr. Horsley Palmer. Various amusements were provided for their entertainment; among others, a grand balloon was sent up. They were not so much astonished by this as was expected, but were greatly delighted with some children who had been invited, of whom they took a great deal of notice. The story of the first visit of a king and queen of the Sandwich Islands to England has a very sad end. They both took measles, and died in London. It is thought that the round of gaiety and sight-seeing of a great city into which they were plunged—so unlike the free, open-air life to which they were accustomed —and the different kind of food they ate, had enfeebled their constitutions, so that when they took the measles they were unable to fight against it. King George sent his own physicians to see them, and everything that could be thought of was done for them, but all in vain. The young queen, only twenty-two years old, died first, after a most touching parting from her husband. He is said to have found comfort in that sad hour from the religion he was only just beginning to know, and that he raised his eyes upwards, and exclaimed, " She is gone to heaven." The separation was not a long one, for the king himself died the following week. The bodies of the young king and queen were taken back to the Sandwich Isles, where the people were all overwhelmed with grief. They were buried at Honolulu, the principal town of the island of Oahu, with all Christian rites. It is wonderful that the death of their king and queen during their short visit to England did not shake the confidence of the Sandwich Islanders in the English nation; but they do not seem to have doubted us. I suppose the members of the suite who had accompanied the royal visitors were able to convince their countrymen of our good faith, and most friendly relations have been kept up between them and us ever since.

Though the Sandwich Islanders have gradually become civilised and Christianised, and have grown, in many ways, like their neighbours and teachers, the Americans, they still retain their own individuality of character and many of their national customs and habits. They are an indolent, pleasure-loving people. Hilo is a sort of holiday house, where the inhabitants seem to give themselves up to the enjoyment of the sunshine, and the delightful air, and the abundant flowers, which bloom all the year round. An intense love of flowers, which they share with so many of the Pacific islanders, is one of their chief characteristics. The girls and women are constantly employed in making wreaths and flower necklaces of every description, with which they adorn themselves. Strangers who land at Hawaii or Oahu are sure of a flowery welcome—lovely garlands of fresh flowers are immediately flung round their necks and heads, till some-

times the weight of them is most inconvenient to the
guests whom the natives delight to honour, and who
do not like to remove them for fear of hurting the
feelings of the kind givers. When Sir Thomas and
Lady Brassey visited Hawaii in their famous yacht,
the *Sunbeam,* they found her, on their return after a day

HAWAIIANS EATING "POI."

on shore, decorated all over with flowers by the kindly
natives. All her masts were tipped with sugar-cane in
bloom. The gangway was surmounted by a triumphal
arch, the whole deck was festooned with tropical plants
and flowers, and in the arms of the figure-head was
an enormous bouquet.

A favourite amusement of the Hawaiians is scam-

VIEW OF LAHAINA.

pering about on horseback, the ladies in gay riding-dresses, which float on each side of them as they ride in manly fashion, which seems to be the only safe way for themselves and their horses to ascend the steep and dangerous bridle-paths round the outskirts of Hilo. Every inhabitant of Hilo has a horse of some description.

The usual Polynesian style of cooking between hot stones still prevails in the Sandwich Islands. The "taro," or "kalo," a sort of arum, forms their principal article of diet, and the energies of the native men are principally spent in cultivating it in pits, which have to be kept constantly watered. Indeed, the finest kind grows entirely in water. There is no plant, except perhaps the banana, which yields so much food, in proportion to the ground it occupies, as the taro. It is said that a pit the size of a very small room will feed a man for a whole year, if it is well cultivated. The root is excellent sliced and simply cooked; but the form in which the natives value it most is when made into a sort of fermented paste, which they call "poi," which is the favourite national dish. The roots are baked in an underground oven, and then pounded with a heavy stone pestle on a slightly hollowed board, which is exceedingly hard and tedious work. When thoroughly pounded, the substance is mixed with water till it becomes a sort of paste, and placed in large calabashes, where it is left for a few days to ferment. By the time it is ready for use, it is nothing but a stiff, sour paste, of a pink or lilac colour, most unattractive to any one but a Hawaiian, but the taste for it may be acquired by perseverance. The Hawaiians, like most of the natives of the Pacific islands, are famous bathers and swimmers. Surf bathing, on boards made from the bread-fruit tree, is quite a national sport, and very exciting in rough weather. Having swum out to some distance with these boards under their arms, they ride over the breakers on them towards the shore, generally lying face downwards, but the most expert bathers kneel, or even stand up on their boards, mounting each roller at the right moment, so as to keep exactly on its curl. They are also wonderful divers.

The place of most importance in the Sandwich Islands, after Honolulu and Hilo, is Lahaina, on the south-west of the island of Moui, which used to be one of the great missionary stations. The harbour is very beautiful. The beach is all made of broken coral, dazzlingly white. The town, like Hilo, is half-buried in the luxuriant tropical foliage, with a line of vivid green at the back, formed by a sugar-cane plantation, and above tower the grand mountains of Eeka. From Lahaina you have a view of the small, mountainous island of Molokai, lovely in the distance, but most sad in its associations, for it is here that all the natives of the Sandwich Islands afflicted with the strange and terrible disease of leprosy are sent. Some years ago it was found necessary, on account of the increase of this disease in the Sandwich Islands, to isolate all those suffering from it, to prevent it spreading more, and if possible to stamp it out entirely. It was a most sad necessity to take all these poor afflicted people from their home and their friends, and at first it was very hard to find them all out and remove them, as they hid themselves, and tried to conceal their complaint as long as possible; but, on account of its frightful and infectious nature, it had to be done. All arrangements

possible for the comfort of these poor creatures were
made by the government, but they know it is an exile
for life—that they can never look upon the faces of
those they love again; and that nothing lies before them
in this world but a lingering death from a hideous
disease, the symptoms and nature of which are too
dreadful to dwell on, separated from all those dear
to them. The only member of this sad community who
is not afflicted like the rest is a good priest, Father
Damiens, a man of education and refinement, who has
chosen to give up all the comforts and enjoyments of
life, all intercourse with cultivated minds, all hope of
advancement in his Church, and all ties of home and
country, and bury himself among these poor lepers. In
the midst of the most painful and distressing sights and
surroundings he lives, always employed in ministering
to the sufferers. Of the many devoted and self-
sacrificing lives of which we have read in the history of
the missions to the islands of the Pacific Ocean, this
seems the most wonderful and beautiful. All those who
know about him, whether Christian or heathen, Roman
Catholic or Protestant, join in their admiration and
reverence for Father Damiens; but he does not look for
such recognition of his work. He does it for the love of
the Master, whose example he is striving to follow, and
whose approval will be his exceeding great reward.

# CHAPTER XI.

## PITCAIRN'S ISLAND, AND THE MARQUESAS.

The First Inhabitants — The Pitcairn Islanders—Their Mode of Living— The Village of Pitcairn—The Resources of the Island too small for its Inhabitants—Descriptions of the Marquesas—The Inhabitants—Tattooing—The Natives' Visitors—Idols of the Natives—Description of Easter Island—Its Inhabitants, and their Mode of Living—Ancient Monuments.

ONLY a hundred years ago, Pitcairn's Island, the name of which and the character of its inhabitants are now so familiar to us, was that most attractive of all places to me when a child—and I suppose to most children—a "desert island." I fancy that most of us who have lived in the country when children—and even some who have only had London squares to run about in, have played at being on a desert island. Certainly all who have read those delightful, but now rather old-fashioned books, "The Swiss Family Robinson," and "Leila," not to speak of "Robinson Crusoe" himself, have done so.

Pitcairn's Island, which is only about six miles long

and three broad, looks like a mere speck in the vast
Pacific Ocean. It is completely iron-bound with rocky
shores, and landing there in boats is always difficult,
though it is safe to approach within a short distance in a
ship. The water is extraordinarily deep close to its very
shores, and it is impossible for ships to anchor there.
But within the rocky precipices round the coast are lovely
valleys with palm forests, and groves of cocoa-nut trees,
and bread-fruit, and the climate is delicious and the soil
rich. The strange romantic story of the white people
who first took possession of this desert island, the
"Mutineers of the Bounty" has been often told, but never
loses its interest and fascination.

Towards the close of the last century, a ship called
the *Bounty* was sent from England to the South Sea
Islands. She was not sent with a view of making
further geographical research, but to get supplies of
young bread-plants from Tahiti, and carry them on to
the West Indies, where the merchants wished to
cultivate them, thinking they would make a valuable
addition to the food of the negroes employed in the
plantations. The *Bounty* was commanded by Lieutenant
Bligh, a man of the most tyrannical and savage temper.
He treated the officers and men under him with contempt
and cruelty, and made their lives a burden to them, even
when they were sailing among those beautiful and sunny
islands. The ship stayed for some little time at Tahiti,
and then sailed again bound for the West Indies, with
upwards of a thousand young bread-fruit trees safely
stored on board. The officer next in command, called
Fletcher Christian, to whom the captain had been
specially insulting, and who had long borne the insults
in respectful silence, brooded and brooded over his

LIEUTENANT BLIGH CAST ADRIFT.

wrongs, till at last he could bear it no longer; and one night, after Lieutenant Bligh had spoken to him in the most ungentlemanly and intolerable manner, a wicked revenge came into his mind. He took several of the seamen into his confidence, who hated the captain with an equally bitter hatred to his own. They armed themselves, and seizing an opportunity when the mate of the morning watch had fallen asleep, and the one who was to relieve him had not yet come on deck, they took possession of the ship and made the captain a prisoner. In vain he expostulated and implored, and reminded them of the crime they were committing against the laws of their country, and how they might have to answer for it with their lives. Christian was inexorable, the launch was lowered, the captain ordered into it, and a certain number of men with him, and it was sent forth, very lightly provisioned, to take its chance on the wide ocean. The history of its voyage and final arrival at the coast of Timor, a distance of 3,618 miles, is wonderfully interesting and marvellous. In reading Lieutenant Bligh's journey, with the descriptions of the frightful sufferings of himself and his crew from hunger, thirst, heat and cold, in that open boat, and his own wonderful skill in navigating it, and making the scanty provisions last out, it is impossible to help sympathising for the time with him, and forgetting how his own evil temper and cruel disposition had brought all this misery on himself and others.

Meanwhile " Mr. Christian," as the crew, who never lost their respect for him, always called him, remained in possession of the ship. All who stayed with him were not by any means mutineers. Two midshipmen called Stewart and Heyward were down in their cabin collecting some clothes to take with them in the boat—fully meaning to stand by the captain—when she was pushed off, being already dangerously low down in the water from the number of men and the weight of the provisions in her. It is terrible to think of what Christian's feelings must have been now that the excitement of his rash and wicked deed was over, and he knew that his only chance of escaping from its terrible consequences was to hide himself and his history for ever. Even if Mr. Bligh had not lived to tell the tale himself, or any of his companions, Christian could never have dared to set foot in his native land again. From that dreadful day forward one would think all peace of mind must have died within him. However, he exerted himself in every way to keep up the spirits of his companions and to find them a safe hiding-place, for he knew full well that should Mr. Bligh ever reach England, a ship would be at once sent out in search of them, to take them prisoners. All the bread-fruit trees were thrown into the sea, and the ship put back to Tahiti, to the delight of all on board, as it was a favourite place with all. The natives welcomed them back again most kindly; but Christian did not remain long there, he wanted to find a safer and less well-known place of retreat. The larger number of the party, however, including those who had no share in the mutiny, and who wished to return home, decided to remain there. Christian advised the midshipmen to give themselves up directly should an English man-of-war appear.

It was of course some time before a ship from England could arrive in search of them, but at length the *Pandora* appeared in the bay of Tahiti, and all the party were taken prisoners. Stewart and Heyward at once gave themselves up, but they were put in irons like the

M

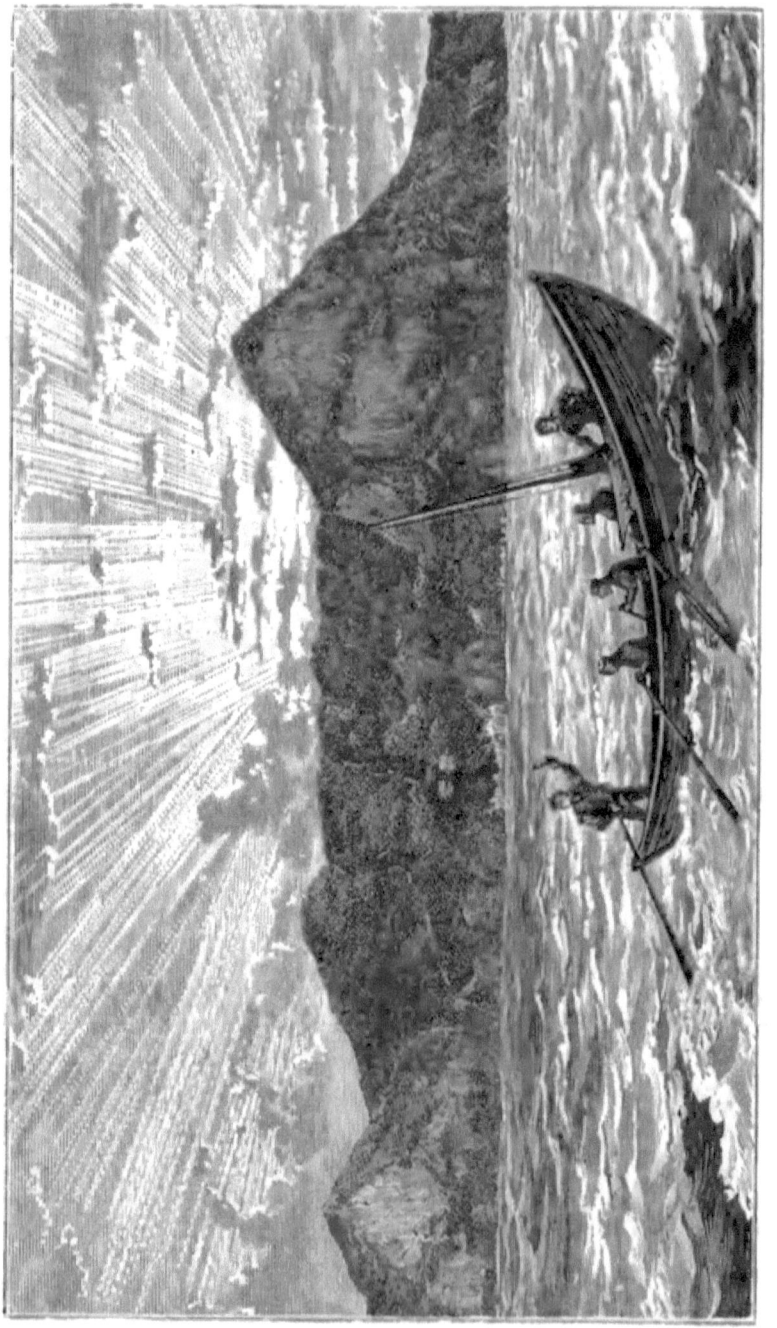

PITCAIRN'S ISLAND.

others, and, owing to the captain being another harsh
and cruel man, suffered every sort of privation and misery.
They were all shut up in a sort of round-house on the
quarter deck, where they had hardly room to breathe.
The contrast of this to the free open-air life they had
been lately leading among the flowers, and the cocoa-nut
trees, and the kindly natives, must have been indeed
dreadful! However, those whose consciences were free
from the crime of which all were suspected had at least
happiness in the thought that they were on their way
home to their friends.

The *Pandora* was wrecked on her way home, and all
had to take to the boats; many were lost, amongst them
several of the prisoners. Those who reached England in
safety were all tried by court-martial, three were hanged,
but those who could prove they had taken no part in the
mutiny were of course pardoned, amongst them young
Heyward, whose history is altogether a most interesting
one.

Pitcairn's Island, of which Christian had read a description, was the place which seemed to him most suitable
for his new home, as being so small and out of the way,
and so difficult of access. There accordingly he sailed,
accompanied, besides his own people, by a number of
Tahitian men and women who were attached to them, and
were most useful to them in many ways. Owing to the
position of Pitcairn's Island having been laid down incor-
rectly in the charts, Christian was many weeks before he
could find it, but at last a solitary-looking rock was
descried in the far distance to the great joy of all, and
soon all on board the *Bounty* had landed on the island,
never to leave its shores again. Christian was delighted
to find the beauty and fertility of the valleys in the in-

M 2

terior of the island, and after making a survey of it, he divided it into nine portions. One he kept for himself, and the other eight were taken possession of by his eight white companions. They had left the ship in a bend in the shore which has ever since borne the name of "Bounty Bay." Here, after removing every article from her that could be of any use, including the planks from her-sides and every nail and bolt, they set fire to her and sank her in twenty-five fathoms of water, that no trace might be left which could ever tell any tales.

The history of the next few years is sad and terrible. The shadow of the crime they had committed seemed to hang about the mutineers, in spite of all their efforts to disperse it in the sunshine of the beautiful tropical island they had made their own. They cultivated the land, and sowed, and planted, and built comfortable wooden huts; but a settled gloom and sadness

THE LANDING-PLACE, BOUNTY BAY.

had taken possession of Christian. He would spend whole days in a cave in the most inaccessible part of the island, and was for ever gazing out over the blue ocean : not with the usual longing of a man cast on a desert island for the sight of a sail rising against the horizon, but in constant fear and dread of it. It is piteous to think of his state of mind, in which his best hope lay in never again hearing of home and friends, and his one remaining object in life to be forgotten by all. As time went on, and no sail appeared, his constant fear of being discovered lessened, but now new troubles arose : disagreements between the white people and the Tahitians they had brought with them. Some of the mutineers had married the Tahitian women, and their wives warned them, in a song, of a plot of their own countrymen against them ; adding these words to the ones they were in the habit of singing : " Why does black man sharpen axe ? To kill white man." This plot was soon frustrated, but it was shortly succeeded by another, and this time Christian was shot dead while working in his garden, and four of the other Englishmen, the rest narrowly escaping with their lives. There were now only four white men left, and as the only means of ensuring their own safety, they decided to kill all the Tahitian men, in which dreadful deed they were assisted by the wives. Even this was not the end of the horrors. Two of the remaining Englishmen found out a way of distilling spirits from a native plant, called the ti root, and took to drinking frightfully ; one threw himself off the cliffs in a fit of drunkenness, and the other became so violent and dangerous, that the remaining two, Smith and Young, determined to put an end to him, in order to secure their own lives.

Nine years had now passed away since the mutineers and their Tahitian companions had landed in Pitcairn's Island, and of them all only two men were left. On their characters, and the principles they chose to inculcate, depended the future of the settlement, for many children, half English and half Tahitian, had been born in the island, who might have been brought up as Christian, or heathen, or in whatever manner these two surviving fathers chose. Happily they realised their strange and important responsibilities, and determined to give up all evil courses, and devote themselves to bringing up the

SCENES IN PITCAIRN'S ISLAND.

children of the island in the fear of God. Young
always attributed the change in his own life to an
extraordinary dream.    He dreamed that the angel
Gabriel came down from heaven, and spoke to
him about his past wickedness, and implored him to
repent; from that time he became a religious man.
Christian had left behind him a Bible and Prayer-book,
both of which he had constantly read, but since his
death they had been neglected.  These were now produced, and daily morning and evening prayers were
established.  Edward Young having had a superior
education to Smith, began the good work of teaching and
training the children, and Smith no doubt improved his
own mind by associating constantly with him.  Young,
however, did not live long, and very soon Smith found
himself the only white man in the island, sole guardian
and teacher to the children springing up round him.
Nothing can be more wonderful and interesting than
the history of this good and wise man, for certainly
whatever were the faults of his early life such he became in every sense of the word.   He seems to have
been father, schoolmaster, lawyer, doctor, and minister
all at once to the Pitcairn Islanders, besides holding
in fact the position of governor of the island.

Twenty years passed away after the Mutiny of the
*Bounty* before anything was known in England about this
strange little community, but at length an American
ship, called the *Topaze*, being short of water, tried to
approach a rocky island, which the captain at first
imagined to be uninhabited.  What was his surprise to
see smoke, and other signs of civilised habitation, as he
came near;   the shore seemed quite inaccessible, but
presently a canoe was seen, and to the surprise of all on

board, voices from it were heard, offering assistance in good English; an English sailor volunteered to go on shore, and the mystery was soon explained, by Alexander Smith himself unfolding the strange history. The captain of the ship landed also on hearing the sailor's report, and was delighted with all he saw of the good order among the islanders, and the atmosphere of peace and prosperity. He related to Smith all the principal events which had taken place in the world during the last twenty years, and when Smith heard of the great naval victories of Trafalgar, and others which England had achieved, he threw his cap into the air and shouted, " Hurrah! Old England for ever!"

The American ship sailed away, and the report of her visit to Pitcairn's Island reached England, and caused great interest and curiosity, which was increased some time later. Two English frigates visited the island together, imagining, owing to the mistake in the position given in the charts, that they were making a new discovery. It was evening when the island was first seen, and the ships could not venture very close, but at daybreak next morning those on board could see through their glasses a number of figures on the rocks watching their proceedings. Two of them had canoes on their shoulders; these were soon launched and paddled through the rough sea to the ships. " Won't you heave us a rope?" cried a young man in one of them, and he had soon sprung on deck, and informed the captain who he was in these words :—

" I am Thursday October Christian, son of Fletcher Christian, the mutineer, by a Tahitian mother, and the first-born on the island." He was a very fine-looking young man, scantily attired, as was usual on the island,

"I AM THURSDAY OCTOBER CHRISTIAN."

and wearing upon his head a hat with a plume of black-cock's feathers in it.    His companion's name was Edward Young; the two young men were both tall and strong, with dark complexions, and long black hair flowing down their shoulders.    They were not in the least shy or awkward, but had pleasant modest manners, and were delighted to be shown over the ship, and deeply inte-rested in all they saw.    When a little black terrier ap-peared, one of them said that he knew that was a dog, he had read of such things.    When they were offered breakfast in the captain's cabin, they repeated a short grace before sitting down, which they said had been taught them by their beloved pastor, John Adams, for Alexander Smith had changed his name after the visit of the American ship, to avoid being recognised, and now called himself John Adams.

The two captains, Sir F. Staines and Captain Pipon, went on shore with the young men, and were introduced to the father of the island, now an elderly man; who stood with his hat in his hand while he talked to them, and smoothed his thin grey locks.    The sight of the familiar naval uniform must have sent a strange thrill through him, half-painful and half-pleasurable, one would think.    He went through all the history of the mutiny, and spoke with sorrow and regret for his part in it, but seemed fully persuaded that he had long ago been for-given by God for it.    He was now spending his life in God's service, and his mind was full of peace and joy. He seemed inclined, however, to return to England, now that the opportunity offered, even at the risk of being tried by the laws of his country, but his children, and all the other inhabitants of the island, were in such despair at the idea of losing him, that the Englishmen felt it would be wrong to take him away from his home and his work. All they saw of these delighted them. The Pitcairn Islanders welcomed them in the warmest manner, caressing them and waiting on them with charming simplicity.

The little village of Pitcairn stood on a rock, in the midst of bananas and banyan trees, and surrounded by glorious scenery. The precipices, which had formerly been so bare, were now clothed with cocoa-nut trees, palms, and bread-fruit trees, down to the water's edge. The little houses were built of wood, generally two stories high, and were very neat and comfortable inside. The farming arrangements were all English, each house having pigstyes, a poultry yard, and a bakehouse. Besides these was a building for the manufacture of cloth, made from the bark of the paper-mulberry, in which the elder women were employed, while the younger ones worked with their fathers and brothers in the plantations of yams and sweet potatoes. Captain Pipon describes all the young people as being tall and handsome, and capital climbers and swimmers. The women wore a loose bodice and skirt down to the ankles, and their long black hair twisted into a graceful knot, without any pin or fastening. They also wore wreaths of sweet-scented flowers, according to the Tahitian fashion. Their food was pork or fowl, baked between stones, as in Tahiti, bread-pudding, made of the Taro root, fruit and vegetables. They drank water, or an infusion of ti-root, sweetened with sugar-cane. After the experiments of his former companions, which had proved so fatal to their health and morals, Adams would never allow spirits to be distilled on the island. All the habits of the islanders were orderly and peaceful. There seemed to be no quarrelling, no discontent. Sunday was kept most strictly as a day of rest, and the children attended the schools regularly.

In the course of time, three different seafaring men left their ships and joined the little community, eventually marrying Pitcairn girls. These men had all more or less education, and were most useful in assisting Adams in his work. The first of them became a schoolmaster, and the last, George Hunn Nobbs, was appointed by John Adams before his death to succeed him in the ministry. He was subsequently ordained a clergyman by the Bishop of London, and for that purpose he came to England, where he was most kindly received by many people interested in the Pitcairn Islanders.

The people of Pitcairn were always delighted when any good wind brought a ship within their reach, and overwhelmed their visitors with kindness and hospitality. Mr. Carleton, the author of a remarkable book on Music, lately published, "The Genesis of Harmony," was once left on the island with four companions for three weeks. They were on their way to San Francisco, in the barque *Noble,* and had landed at Pitcairn, with the intention of exploring the island, and to their consternation their ship, for some reason never satisfactorily explained, sailed away without them. They were most kindly entertained and provided for by the islanders, and were greatly pleased and interested in all they saw of them. Mr. Carleton lived in John Adams' house. Finding them singing hymns with unusually fine voices, but only in unison and in most rudimentary style, he set to work at once to teach them notes, with a black board and a piece of chalk, in Mr. Hullah's fashion. He began on a Friday, and his pupils were so interested

in their work, and so clever at it, that by Monday they
were singing the quaint old catch—

> " My wife's dead, there let her lie,
>   She's at rest, and so am I ; "

keeping their parts quite correctly.  Their progress
during the three weeks was wonderful.  At the end of
that time Mr. Carleton and his friends were picked up
by a ship bound for San Francisco, and borne away from
the simple-hearted islanders, after the most affectionate
embraces, amidst a chorus of lamentation.  They could
scarcely have left behind them a more valuable legacy
than the elements of music, which the Pitcairners
followed up most industriously, Mr. Carleton having
written out for them a number of glees and rounds.  It
is pleasant and interesting to think of the writer of a
learned work on music, representing a lifetime of
musical study, having used the most elementary part of
his knowledge in this manner; and it must, I should
think, be a great pleasure to him to notice in all
accounts of the Pitcairn Islanders and their doings,
special mention of their excellent part-singing.  Mrs.
Carleton amused me much by telling us that once, in
looking over a certain little drawer of her husband's, she
came upon a quantity of dark, coarse-looking hair of
different shades, which she took for horsehair at first,
but which proved to be precious locks presented to him
by the Pitcairn young ladies on his departure !

Good John Adams' death occurred in 1829, and was
a terrible loss and grief to the islanders ; but they continued to bring up their children in all the good ways
he had taught them.

As the population increased, the resources of the

(1.)—SCHOOL AND CHAPEL BUILT BY JOHN
ADAMS.  (2.)—GRAVE OF ADAMS.

island be-
came too
small for its
inhabitants, and they
were persuaded by
the British Govern-
ment to remove to
Tahiti.  They were
not happy there, how-
ever, and soon went
back again.  In 1856
they were removed
to Norfolk Island,
and there the greater
part of them remain
still; but a small
portion became so
home-sick that they
made their way back
once more to Pitcairn's Island.

The last I have heard about the Pitcairn Islanders is

in a simple and very interesting account of "A Trip to
Norfolk Island," in November, 1880, written by a
young lady in New Zealand, and published in the May
number of a monthly magazine. The occasion of
the visit was the opening and consecration of the
Memorial Chapel of St. Barnabas to Bishop Patteson,
first Bishop of the Melanesian Mission, to which this
lady and her father were invited. To have such a
beautiful chapel attached to his college of St. Barnabas
was one of Bishop Patteson's greatest wishes during his
lifetime, and its fulfilment, as one of the fruits of his
death ten years ago at the hands of the natives of
Nukapu, has a joyful as well as a sad interest.

The New Zealand visitors received a hearty welcome
from the present bishop of the mission, and all the
people of the island. A visit to Mr. Nobbs, the
venerable pastor of the Pitcairners, now Norfolk
Islanders, is specially mentioned. It was one of his
sons, Edwin, who, with Fisher Young, was killed by
the poisoned arrows of the natives of Santa Cruz, when
visiting it with Bishop Patteson, to his intense grief.
"We saw Bishop Patteson's room," this lady writes,
"which he describes so cheerily in his letters to his
sisters; and there over the mantelshelf is the copy of
Leonardo da Vinci's 'Last Supper' just as it hung
when he was there; and many of his other things are
still about; the boys slipping in and out just as they
used to do in his time; and from the broad verandah
the beautiful view of Mount Pitt's forest-covered slopes
which he used to look at." Then follows a description
of the church, and the consecration service.

The church was crowded, and English, Maories,
Melanesians, and Norfolk Islanders all joined in singing

"The Church's One Foundation." The service was conducted in the Mota language, which is the one always spoken at the college. A beautiful prayer was specially offered, in which thanks to God were given "for the life and death of thy servant, John Coleridge Patteson, first Bishop of this Mission, in whose memory we now dedicate this church to Thee, and for the example of those who died with him." Many others connected with this mission are mentioned, amongst them " the children of this island, Edwin Nobbs and Fisher Young, who, wounded at Santa Cruz, were content 'doing their duty ' to die in Thy service."

No wonder the Norfolk Islanders love and reverence the memory of these two young men. One cannot read of their gentle, loving dispositions, their unselfish lives, and the christian resignation with which they met their cruel deaths, without feeling that the examples they have left are among the fairest flowers of the good seed sown by the repentant mutineer in the rocky island.

The group of islands called the "Marquesas" was named in honour of a Spanish marquis, who discovered them in 1595. The islands are very numerous, and vary in size from ten to twenty miles. They are not encircled or protected by coral reefs, though there is plenty of coral to be seen on the beach; the coast is very rocky and abrupt, but there are many good harbours, such as Resolution Bay in Tahuata, which is a particularly fine and safe one. All the usual fruits and plants of the South Seas grow there, and the climate is warm, but very healthy. The inhabitants belong to the same race as those of the Society and Sandwich Islands. They have dark, copper-coloured skins; but that of the women is much paler than of the men. They are said to have wonderfully beautiful figures; and one navi-

A TATTOOED CHIEF OF THE MARQUESAS ISLANDS.

gator describes a chief the measurements of whose body
agreed exactly with those of the Apollo Belvedere. 1

N.

think, however, that the tattooing with which he was
adorned must have entirely destroyed the resemblance
to the Apollo. This art is carried to a greater degree of
perfection in the Marquesas Islands than in any other
nation. The bodies of distinguished persons are com-

NATIVE OF THE MARQUESAS.

pletely covered with regular figures in most tasteful and
elaborate patterns; and this process makes their skin
darker than it would be otherwise. The women, who
are nearly as fair as Europeans, and very beautiful, do
not often disfigure themselves in this way.

There is a delightful old-fashioned book by Hermann

A WARRIOR OF THE MARQUESAS ISLANDS.

N 2

Melville, which describes his four months' residence
there in so lifelike a manner, that after reading it one
really feels as if one had been living there too. The
author, who went by the name of Tommo among the natives, was a sailor, who, accompanied by his friend Toby,
left his ship the *Dolly*, which had put into the harbour
of one of these islands for a few days, and hid till she
had sailed. These two young men were so miserable on
board this ship that they determined to brave everything,
even being eaten by the natives, of some of whom they
had heard terrific accounts, rather than remain in her.
They were obliged to hide in a valley till the ship was
fairly gone, living in the utmost misery, drenched
by heavy rains, and with only a few biscuits to eat;
and when at last they ventured to show themselves
to the natives, were in fear of their lives. However,
they were most kindly and hospitably received. The
noble-looking chief Mehevi took them under his special
protection; and poor Tommo, having seriously injured
his leg in his climbs, was provided with a most kind
and attentive valet to wait on him, called Kory-Kory.
This kind savage used to carry him down to the water,
every day to bathe, on his back. Tommo and Toby
lived in a bamboo hut with a large family of natives.
The furniture of the hut consisted of two long well-
polished trunks of the cocoa-nut tree, extending the
whole length of the building, two yards apart. The
space was filled up with gaily-worked mats of different
patterns, on which all the inhabitants of the hut
lounged and slept. From the ridge-pole which supported the house hung various packages wrapped up in
tapa; festival dresses, and other valuable articles.

The warrior chief Mehevi was dressed in a very

elaborate manner. Brilliant feathers of tropical birds formed an upright semicircle on his head, supported in a crescent of guinea-beads. Round his neck were several enormous necklaces of boars' tusks, polished like ivory. In his ears he wore whales' teeth, the hollow parts being turned to the front, and filled with freshly-plucked leaves, with little images hanging to them. He had a short skirt of dark-coloured tapa hanging before and behind, in clusters of braided tassels, and anklets and bracelets of curling human hair. In one hand he held a beautifully-carved spear, nearly fifteen feet high, and a richly-decorated pipe, with its stem stained a bright red, hung from his girdle, with streams of thin white tapa fluttering round it. Mehevi was tattooed all over in wonderful and intricate patterns like lace-work.

The Marquesas women are very simply and gracefully dressed in tunics of snow-white tapa, and mantles of the same, when exposed to the sun, with necklaces and flowers strung together on fibres of tapa, bracelets and anklets made in the same way, and garlands of flowers on their heads. Hermann Melville describes one charming young girl, called Fayaway, dressed in this manner, who he says was the perfection of grace and beauty. She had a clear olive skin, dazzling white teeth, and dark brown hair which fell over her shoulders in natural curls. Fayaway lived in the same house with him, as well as a nice old man and his wife, the parents of Kory-Kory. The old lady was always bustling about, waiting on everybody; cooking the funny native dishes, different preparations of bread-fruit and cocoa-nuts, and racing off into the valley to fetch herbs and leaves for different purposes. The natives became so attached to their visitors that they would not let them go, when reports of a ship in sight

BOY AND IDOL OF THE MARQUESAS.

reached them. Toby, however, one day disappeared, but his friend was never satisfied about him; he could not believe he would willingly have deserted him, and was always **haunted** with the **idea that he had** met with foul **play.** **When** poor Tommo **found himself quite** alone among the natives, he fell into very low spirits indeed; however, his hosts did **all they** could **to cheer and** amuse him, and at the end of **four** months he managed **to escape.** He was happy **with them on the** whole, but knowing the fickleness **of** savage nature never felt sure that they might not take it into their heads to kill and eat him. It is difficult to believe, however, in reading the description of the devotion **of** Kory-Kory, that he would ever have changed **to him in such a** manner. Once in the middle **of the** night **Tommo and** Toby were dreadfully frightened by the natives getting up, and making a great fire **outside the hut; the** unpleasant idea came into their minds, and **was** not to **be** dispelled for some time, that the object **of** this sudden fire at so strange an hour was **to** cook them! At length, however, two of the natives stole softly in with a large trencher full of steaming meat, **and the** words "Tommo, Toby, ki, ki, (eat, eat)." They had been roasting **a pig for** a midnight feast, and wished the sleeping **visitors to** have **a** share.

The **idols of these people are very rough,** clumsy **things, and though they believe** them **to** have great **power, they** do not always treat them with much respect. **The Typees, among** which tribe Tommo was living, had **a baby god, of whom** they thought a great deal, called Moa **Atua ; it looked** like **a** bit of a broken war club with a rough human head carved at one **end,** and was swathed round in scarlet and white tapa, and carried in the arms of the chief priest. This is the funny sort of ceremony they go through. The priest caresses and dandles Moa Atua, and whispers in its car; when it makes no answer he appears to get provoked, and bawls to it; no answer being vouchsafed still, he gets apparently very angry indeed, strips the baby god of its finery, and buries it in a hole. By-and-bye he takes it out again, whispers once more, and then informs the bystanders of various interesting communications which it has made to him, and which they firmly believe. Kory-Kory told his English friend that if Moa Atua were so minded, he could cause a cocoa-nut to sprout out of his head, and that it would be the easiest thing in the world for him to take the whole island in his mouth, and dive to the bottom of the sea with it.

All the natives of the Marquesas Islands are splendid swimmers, and pass a great deal of their time in the water, splashing and diving about. Among the Typees canoes were tabooed to women, so if they wanted to get from one place to another, they were forced to swim. The mothers put their babies into the water soon after they are born, and let go of them for a minute or two at a time, and by being launched in this manner, like little ducks, they soon swim of their own accord. Of course, the water is very nice and warm in this part of the world, so that it is only like being put into a large warm bath, which babies always like, and not at all the same thing as being plunged into the cold rough sea by a bathing-woman in England, which they certainly don't enjoy.

Easter Island is a very remote and rather dreary little island, some thirty or forty miles round. It is so named, because it lies eastward of all the islands of the

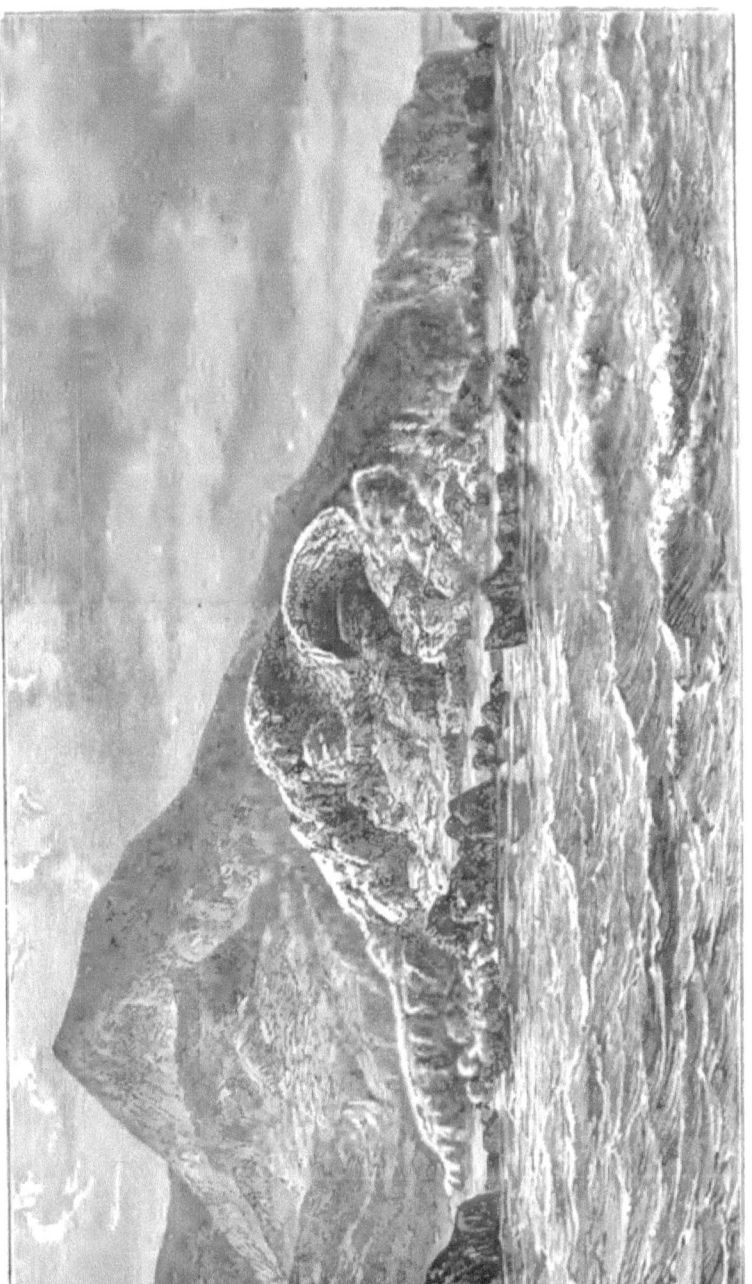

EASTER ISLAND.

South Pacific Ocean.   Pitcairn is its nearest neighbour
of any consequence.   It has a stony and hilly surface,
and an iron-bound shore.   At the south of the island
there is an extinct volcano, and the hills seem to be
chiefly formed of lava.   There is no safe anchorage at
Easter Island, no wood for fuel, no fresh water, and no
domestic animals, except a few fowls.   The inhabitants
live on yams, potatoes, and sugar-cane, the soil being so
exceedingly fertile that three days' work is sufficient to
provide sustenance for a native for a whole year.   No
wonder that the inhabitants of these regions are inclined
to be idle, and take things as easily as possible.

The early missionaries and settlers of these islands
tell us that often when they tried to get the natives
to build more comfortable houses and adopt different
modes of civilised life, they would answer, " We
should like some of these things very well, but we
cannot have them without working; that we do not
like, and therefore would rather do without them.
The bananas and the plantains ripen on the trees, and
the pigs fatten on the fruits that are strewed beneath
them, even while we sleep ; these are all we want, why
therefore should we work ? "

Lord Byron has expressed this idea most poetically,
and at the same time graphically :

> " They knew no higher, sought no happier state,
>   Had no fine instinct of superior joys.
>   Why should they toil to make the earth bring forth,
>   When without toil she gave them all they wanted?
>   The bread-fruit ripened, while they lay beneath
>   Its shadows in luxurious idleness ;
>   The cocoa filled its nuts with milk and kernels,
>   And while they slumbered from their heavy meals
>   In dead forgetfulness of life itself ;

The fish were spawning in unsounded depths,
The birds were breeding in adjacent trees,
The game was fattening in delicious pastures,
Unplanted roots were thriving **underground**
To spread the **tables** of their future **banquets**."

The natives of Easter Island are fair Polynesians, resembling those of Tahiti and the Marquesas, but they are said to be occasionally cannibals. They make long low houses, something like a canoe turned upside down, with a small opening at the side which serves for door and window; but there are much better and more interesting houses than these in the island built of stone, about which the present inhabitants know nothing. Easter Island is celebrated for the wonderful remains of some prehistoric people, who must have lived there ages before the race who now inhabit it, and about whom the people there now cannot tell us anything at all. The remains consist of these stone houses, sculptured stones, and gigantic stone images. The houses are built in regular lines, with doors facing the sea, the walls are five feet thick and nearly six feet high, they are built of layers of irregularly-shaped flat stone, and lined inside with upright flat slabs. These are painted with figures of birds and animals, chiefly fabulous creatures (for quadrupeds are little known in Easter Island), and geometrical figures. Quantities of a particular kind of shell were found inside the houses, and in one of them a statue eight feet high was discovered, which is now in the British Museum; it weighs four tons. Near these houses the rocks on the brink of the sea-cliffs are carved into all sorts of strange shapes, sometimes like odd human faces, and sometimes like turtles. There are hundreds of these carvings, often overgrown with bushes and grass of a very coarse rank

VIEW IN EASTER ISLAND.

kind which grows over the island.    But the most extraordinary of these ancient remains are found on nearly
every headland round the coast, where there is almost
always an enormous platform of stone, more or less in
ruins.    Towards the sea there are high walls built of
immense stones most ingeniously fitting into one another

CARVED MONUMENTS ON EASTER ISLAND.

without cement, and within stone platforms and terraces
have been levelled with large slabs which have been
pedestals for the images, now thrown down in all directions and more or less broken to pieces.    One of the
most perfect of these platforms had fifteen images on
it. Most of these statues were as much as fifteen or eigh-
teen feet high, and some as much as thirty-seven feet.

ANCIENT MONUMENTS, EASTER ISLAND.

The figures are human bodies without legs, the heads being flat to allow of crowns being put on : these crowns were made of a red material found only at a crater about three miles from the stone houses. At this place there still remain numbers of these crowns, some of them ten feet round, waiting to be removed to the heads for which they were intended. How it was that they were never placed on these heads, what brought this strange work suddenly to an end, or who were the people engaged in it, we do not know, and shall probably never find out. A certain stone implement, a long pebble with a chisel edge, is believed to have been the chief tool used in making these wonderful statues, but it is almost impossible to believe that with this alone such gigantic works could have been executed in such numbers and in such a small island, isolated from the rest of the world.

A FALLEN MONUMENT IN EASTER ISLAND.

The difficulty is so great that some **writers** believe that there may have been once a **civilisation** over the Pacific Ocean of which neither we nor the inhabitants we found there have ever heard or know anything. Possibly Easter Island may have been **a** sacred spot to all the islands round, and different tribes may have combined **together to** erect these wonderful images there, and may **have worshipped them** as their gods. But nothing is **known for** certain, and Easter Island remains the greatest mystery of the Pacific Ocean.

THE END.

CASSELL, PETTER, GALPIN & CO., BELLE SAUVAGE WORKS, LONDON, E.C.